CHRONICLES
OF THE
KINGDOM
BOOK 1 THE INVITATION

Dianne Joy

Chronicles of the Kingdom: The Invitation

Trilogy Christian Publishers A Wholly Owned Subsidiary of Trinity Broadcasting Network

2442 Michelle Drive Tustin, CA 92780

Manufactured in the United States of America

10 9 8 7 6 5 4 3 2 1

Library of Congress Cataloging-in-Publication Data is available.

ISBN: 978-1-63769-618-7

E-ISBN: 978-1-63769-619-4

Everyone wants a great adventure, and everyone needs a tribe of friends. Open the cover of this magical tale and get swept away by Dianne as she weaves the story of Alli's metamorphosis.

Alli's story reflects the author's heart for the generations to come, as well as her desire for their spiritual freedom. Dianne has filled each page with magic, adventure, and friendship.

Life is a journey toward the kingdom, and the journey truly is our great adventure! I'm smiling as I imagine you turning the pages of Chronicles of the Kingdom Book 1 The Invitation. I know you'll enjoy it as much as I did!

Traci Lynn Fiaretti
Author: Hope Speaks, Whimsie, and Winzo.

DEDICATION

To my children, their children, and the children of the
world. Imagination's spark is the essence of life.
Let yours live!

ACKNOWLEDGMENTS

The truth is we cannot accomplish what we are meant to without the brushstrokes of the Creator, the greatest artist of us all, upon our lives. He welcomes us to join Him and watch as He lovingly places a brush in our clumsy hands and invites us to make something beautiful with Him. Then He surrounds us with a community allowing us to complete the task at hand.

To my community of family and friends who supported and provided feedback for me and this project. I could not have done it without you! Thank you!

My darlin' husband, Glenn, thank you for your love and support. You made this book possible!

Priscilla Sawyer, thank you for believing in Alli, hanging on every word as the story unfolded, and cheering us on. Thank you, Doris Guerrant, for editing this work in its roughest form. You taught me to write better. A special thank you for your time and love in visiting me when I needed it most. Jennifer and daughters, Lily and Lila, my first practice kids to read this work: thank you for your enthusiasm! Traci Fiaretti, my fellow author, your expertise and input into my journey were invaluable. My lovely granddaughter Natalia Love: thank you for helping me (with every word) make sure the kidspeak was relatable. Lindsay Cheek, your contribution is priceless. Your illustrations captured Alli and her journey perfectly! Shawn Bair: thank you for your sacrifice of time and your beautiful edits. Your passion for words painting a picture on a page drew out the best in me, and what you gave to this story is invaluable.

All of you are in my heart forever!

MAIN CHARACTERS IN ORDER OF APPEARANCE

Alli

Mom

Rhey

The snake and the daimons

Saraiyah or Ima

Rose

Prince Trueheart

Raven

Prince Boqer Aster

Dylan

Andrew

Thomas or Tom

HOW TO PRONOUNCE CHARACTER NAMES

Alli [al–lee]

Rhey [ray]

Daimons [day–monz]

Saraiyah [sa–ray–ah]

Ima [e–ma]

Prince Boqer prince [bo–kare]

Raven[ray–vun]

Prince Trueheart prince [tru–hart]

Sir Reynold sir [rayn–nold]

Dylan [di–lon]

Andrew [an–dru]

Thomas [tom–us]

THE INVITATION

As soon as the door slammed behind me, I heard, "Alli?"

"Yeah, Mom, it's me."

"You've got mail!" Mom sounded so excited.

"Really? Me? I have mail?"

"Yes, I think it might be an invitation to a special event or party!"

"Really? For me?"

How was that possible? My mind was racing. I was thirteen years old and never invited to anything! I was definitely *not* the kinda kid who got mail. I knew it was because I was too short and fat with tons of freckles! Plus, the worst part, my hair was *bright red*! I was positive no boy had ever looked at me except with disgust. Added to that, I was so shy and awkward, cringed just being around other kids. I hated all the uncomfortable situations I found myself in. You know, typical stuff at school like PE, choir, lunch, recess, forced group activities, etcetera. Even my first day of school was a nightmare! I was petrified of going to kindergarten! Have you ever heard of anyone being scared to death of kindergarten? No? Me either. But I was! And then, there are friends or, in my case, the lack of friends. Oh, I tried to have them. I even got close once, but then we moved for my mom's work. I used to dream I would have them someday, but honestly, I knew it would never happen: I couldn't have a real friend.

I went to Mom's office door and asked, "Where's the letter, Mom?"

Mom's face was shining with a huge smile. "Will you wait a minute, honey? I want to watch you open it."

"Sure, I'll wait for you."

How could I say no? I wanted Mom to be there for this once-in-a-lifetime event.

Since I had a few minutes to kill, I ran to the kitchen and raided the cookie jar. Mmmm! The sweetness of the chocolate chips tasted so good as they melted in my mouth. Few things were that good! Yeah, food was my true source of comfort as far back as I could remember. I liked to eat! What was wrong with that? There was nothing in life I enjoyed as much as food, which was probably why I was so fat. Who cares? No one liked me anyway, except Mom, of course.

After my dad died when I was three, it's just been Mom and me. Mom's okay, I guess. I know she loves me, but sometimes she's just too perfect! She was pretty: she had a cute turned-up nose, a tiny waist, and honey-blond hair.

Mom never yelled or got mad at me. She was such a nice person, like literally nice to everyone. Everyone!

I munched on my cookie and remembered the stranger who came up to us at the grocery store a few days ago. He told my mom a sob story about his life, and she bought it! Not only that: she even gave him fifteen bucks. Our last fifteen bucks! The money was supposed to buy us lunch, a lunch I earned from finishing my chores and making it to school on time. Neither of those things was easy for me to accomplish, so she was taking me out for a treat. But then, this homeless guy came over, and *boom*! She gave away my reward. Just like that! She saw the look on my face and apologized, but only after she pointed out his troubles.

"I'm sorry, honey. How can we eat out when this man cannot afford to eat at all? I'll make it up to you. Let's go home, and I'll bake your favorite cookies." How could I stay mad at her after that, I ask you?

"Okay!" Mom called excitedly. "I'm ready. Let's open the invitation."

I put down my cookie and rushed to her office.

On her desk laid the invitation. At first, the unusual envelope looked somewhat whitish, but as I moved closer, the color changed. Iridescent blues, pinks, yellows, greens, and purples—rainbow colors flashed and sparkled from the envelope like translucent fairy wings.

"Wow!" I exhaled with curious excitement.

"It's calligraphy," Mom said as I stared at the gold lettering.

Who would send such a fancy invitation? Carefully, I picked up the delicate envelope and tried to figure out how to open it. Was there a tab? Puzzled, I moved in closer. Suddenly, as if by magic, the envelope opened.

"Mom! Did you see that?"

"Uh-huh," she smiled and nodded.

Awestruck, we wondered what would happen next. Then, right before our eyes…Poof! The envelope disappeared—completely. Shocked by what just happened, we stared at each other in disbelief. The envelope was gone, but in its place…right there…in my hand, lay a beautifully handwritten invitation.

To the one who holds this invitation:

You are cordially invited to join us

on the greatest adventure of all.

Come at midnight three days hence,

when your escort comes knocking for you.

With best regards and warmest welcome,

The King of kings

"Mom? Who's the King of kings?" I asked innocently.

"Believe it or not, I know who He is, *and* I know about His kingdom," she replied with a twinkle in her eye.

"You do?" My jaw dropped. I couldn't hide my surprise.

"Alli, you've just received the best invitation! All other

invitations in your life will pale compared to this one."

"Mom? You're not going to let me go, are you?" I asked nervously.

Mom smiled, pursed her lips, and paused before she replied. She knew that would get my attention; it always did. Why was she acting so weird?

"Alli, this is *your* invitation. Just remember, if you decide to go, I know you will be safe, *but* you will be forever changed."

Forever changed? What was she talking about? I guess being changed wasn't a bad idea. The fact was I didn't like myself the way I was, so what could be the harm in changing? Things could only get better. Right?

"Alli," she looked at me knowingly, "everyone has to decide whether or not they want to grow up or stay a child." She chuckled lightly, "An adventure like this will be a challenge. You will grow from your experience."

"Mom, what kind of event starts at midnight? Isn't that when carriages turn back to pumpkins, and beautiful clothes turn back to rags?" The whole thing made me nervous. With my luck, I would turn into a big fat pumpkin. Me getting bigger: *that* would be my great adventure.

"Well," Mom said reassuringly, "your journey will happen while you sleep."

While I was asleep? Had my mom lost her marbles? Things were getting crazier by the minute. First off, the only invitation I'd ever gotten in my whole life was clearly from

Mars or Venus or Jupiter: somewhere out of this world! Then there was my mom, talking about midnight sleep adventures and magic invitations like they were ordinary things…like she was asking me to pick up milk on the way home from school. Where was the simple, stable, loving mother I knew? She never did anything out of the ordinary. She was nice but boring. I liked boring; it was predictable, steady, and safe! Honestly, I didn't know what to think.

"Alli, did you see the note at the bottom of the invitation?"

"What note?"

"The small print here." She pointed to the bottom of the invitation.

How did I miss the bright red letters before?

The invitee has until midnight three days hence to accept or decline this invitation.

If the bearer chooses not to accept, this invitation will expire, and the invitee will miss this opportunity to attend the Great Banquet of the King.

"Banquet of the King? Huh?" I grew even more confused.

"The Banquet is the final event, at the end of the journey."

Mom leaned toward me and spoke softly. She had my full attention. "Alli, you have been invited to the greatest banquet that will ever be given, but you can't attend until you accept the invitation and embark on the journey."

I didn't understand everything she said, but I definitely

liked the idea of a banquet. My love of food warmed my feelings about it all. After all, a banquet couldn't be that bad, could it?

"How do you know about all of this?"

"Well, I haven't always been a mom, you know?" she chuckled. "I was a girl once too. I received my invitation and went on this adventure when I was a little younger than you."

"You did? What was it like?"

"It was unlike anything I have ever experienced. It was the hardest but most wonderful experience of my life. I can't tell you very much about it right now."

Why couldn't she tell me more about her journey? She was acting so strange.

Then, as if she knew what I was thinking, "I can't tell you any more about my experience because yours will be completely unique. No two journeys are alike. Experiences may have similarities, but none are the same. You will have a guide who knows exactly how to lead you. Your journey, like your invitation, is meant only for you. In fact, I couldn't have opened your invitation even if I wanted to. Did you notice it opened when *you* looked at it?"

"Yeah, I guess." I was still a bit confused.

"The invitation scanned your eyes to verify your identity. You…and only you…could open the invitation."

"It scanned my eyes? Like a spy show?"

"Yes!" Mom enthused. "Alli, what feature do you like best about yourself?"

"Oh, Mom," I groaned. "You know I hate thinking about my features." I figured out a long time ago the less I thought about my looks, the less depressed I got.

I considered her question. Even though I disliked almost everything about myself, I liked my eyes. They were pretty. Most redheads had green or blue eyes, but mine were unique: honeyed amber with gold flecks. My mom's stare persisted. I knew she expected a response, so I took a deep breath, let it out slowly, and confessed.

"My eyes. I like my eyes."

"Isn't it funny," Mom grinned, "your favorite feature is what opened the invitation?"

"Yeah, I guess." But I thought it was weird.

"What do you like about your eyes?"

"Well, not many people have my eye color. It makes me feel kinda special, in a good way. I guess."

"Exactly! Your eyes are unique and so very beautiful." She stared intently. "Just like the girl who sees through them."

Oh, brother! Now she was just being Mom!

"If you choose to go, I will support you." She gently lifted my chin, which forced me to look directly into her eyes. "Alli, I believe in you."

All the talk about journeys, guides, midnight banquets, and my mom's unbreakable stare were too much for me. Too much! I couldn't handle it anymore.

"Okay! Thanks, Mom!" I grabbed the invitation and headed to my room.

What was I going to do? Was any of the stuff even real? I tossed the invitation on my desk, wanting to dismiss it. I was done thinking about it. So, I did what any normal thirteen-year-old would do: ate more cookies and started my dreaded math homework. After a few minutes, I put it all behind me and forgot about it until…

STRANGE NIGHTS

As soon as my head hit the pillow, I was asleep. I had the strangest dream. Unlike the too-much-pizza or the late-night-snack weird dreams, the dream took strange to a whole new level.

The full moon peeked in and out of billowy, navy blue clouds, making it hard to see in the darkness. I didn't know what lay ahead of me on the path but sensed there was something up ahead I wanted. Surprisingly, I didn't care how far I'd have to go to get it. Typically, you couldn't get me to do much of anything physical because it usually involved people. But in my dream, I wasn't going to let my plump, couch-potato body hold me back.

Suddenly, a thick bluish fog rolled in, sparkling and swirling with soft iridescence like the invitation. Although I could only see a few feet in front of me, I continued down the path with surprising confidence. I felt very relaxed, even when I noticed someone behind the bushes, quietly walking in step with me. I probably should have been scared, but I wasn't. I kept walking, and they kept walking.

Neither of us spoke. Then just as quickly as the fog rolled in…it lifted, and I awoke.

Lying in bed half-awake, I realized the strangest thing about the dream was me, the way I felt. I wasn't afraid of the darkness or the stranger in my dream. My anxieties and fears had vanished. I felt calm…peaceful-like. It didn't make any sense to me. Did the dream have something to do with the invitation or the journey Mom told me about? I lay there in a cocoon of calm and drifted back to sleep.

In the morning, I was startled awake and looked at the clock. Oh no, I overslept! In a panic, I hurriedly got ready, grabbed a piece of toast, yelled goodbye to Mom, and ran off to school. All day, I had a nagging feeling I'd forgotten something important. My backpack? No, silly, it was on my back! My homework? No, thankfully, it was in my binder. Library book? No, it wasn't due for another week. My lunch? Oh no, not my lunch! I freaked out for a minute and frantically rummaged my locker. Whew! Found it! You would be right if you thought I'd never, *ever* forget my lunch! What the heck had I forgotten? I decided to figure it out later, but I soon forgot about the "forgotten something" feeling as the day rolled by.

After school, I greeted Mom, grabbed my after-school snack (my trusty cookies and a glass of milk), and headed to my room. An overwhelming science project was due in three weeks, and I had procrastinated long enough. It was time to get going on it. I got so lost in the project that the afternoon and evening flew by. I only stopped once…for dinner, of course. The next thing I knew, it was time for PJs, teeth, kiss for Mom…the usual bedtime stuff. After finishing my routine, I climbed into my comfy bed, turned off the light, and closed my eyes.

Within a few minutes, as I was drifting off to sleep, a light shone in my room. I figured it was just my mom making her usual bedtime rounds. She would tuck in my blankets and give me a good night kiss.

"Yeah, Mom!" I grumbled, keeping my eyes closed. "I'm asleep!"

There was no reply, so I peeked through my lashes. Mom wasn't standing there. Where was the light coming from? I looked around my room and noticed a faint glow coming from my desk. Was the invitation glowing? The invitation! Right then, it hit me: the invitation was the thing I'd forgotten all day. Why had it bugged me so much? I didn't know, but maybe because I'd never gotten an invitation in my life! Duh! Plus, the invitation felt special somehow.

I sat up in bed and leaned closer to study the invitation. The faint glow was getting brighter. Why was it glowing? I went to the desk to check it out. The gold letters were pulsing with light like they were alive. As I stared in disbelief, a whole miniature world unfolded: animals and children played while angels and fairies flew overhead. The scene looked like a miniature 3D movie playing right before my eyes. Oh my gosh! I had never seen anything like it.

Curiously, I reached out to pick it up, but the light and scene disappeared as soon as I touched it. As if a book slammed shut. A sense of calm swept over me as I stared at the invitation. I couldn't explain why I felt that way! No surprise, though: lately, I couldn't explain a lot of things. The feeling reminded me of sipping hot cocoa by the fireside while Mom read to me. Warm and cozy, yes, that's what it was.

So many different things had happened since the invitation's arrival: weird dreams, light shows, you name it. Would there be more weird dreams? Or would I wake up and realize none of it was real? Was it all a crazy dream? I couldn't handle thinking I'd wake up and discover my world was still normal and boring. So, I closed my eyes and went to sleep.

THE DREAM UNFOLDS

Once asleep, I found myself on a path again; everything around me was familiar. It was the same path as the night before! The moon, the path, the fog…everything was the same. I looked around and sensed the same person behind the bushes, walking in step with me. After a few minutes, the fog cleared. A rabbit ran ahead of me while a deer leaped over the path. Why weren't the animals asleep? Shouldn't they be in their burrows for the night or something?

In the distance, a little boy strolled along with a lion and lamb behind him. It looked like he was leading them somewhere. I thought it was really weird: the lion was leaving the lamb alone. Were they talking to each other? Talking animals? My mind was full of questions as a deep reverberating laugh from the lion shook the ground. Suddenly, the lamb spun around, closed his eyes, and raised his front hooves to the sky. He was dancing with the biggest smile on his face. He jumped around as if he was at a dance festival. The action didn't stop there. The boy clapped and sang a tune. The words of his song floated toward me.

"Joy, joy, joy,

I've got this joy.

In all the world, there's no other joy,

Like this joy given me.

Joy, joy, joy,

I am so loved and free!"

Captivated by the scene in front of me, I watched intently as the small group disappeared around the bend. As I stood, hoping they would reappear, something in the distance caught my eye. Billowy, navy blue clouds gave way to the full moon, which shone in the distance, like a spotlight, over the most magnificent mountain. How hadn't I noticed the huge mountain before? Reflected hues of violet, blue, grey, and pink danced around the mountain, while hints of gold and silver flickered in the night sky. The glowing vibrance and movement of the colors made the mountain look alive, creating a scene more beautiful than anything I could have imagined.

A grand castle, like a beautiful crown, sat atop the mountain, filling the entire peak. Were the child, lion, and lamb heading there? The bluish fog and navy blue clouds rolled in slowly as I stared at the castle. Was this the castle I'd been invited to? Would the King's banquet be held there? No, I quickly concluded. The invitation was real, and the castle was part of a dream, a beautiful, magnificent dream. What if the castle was real and the invitation was a dream? Questions swam around in my head. Was I losing my mind? Just as I started to panic, I looked around and noticed beside the path, behind the bushes, the person was still there. In an instant, calm and peace washed over me. I breathed it in deeply, and as I exhaled, the dream faded.

Wow! What a dream. Like the previous dream, I awoke filled with peace, but more intensely this time. I took another deep breath and let it out slowly. It felt so good, like my science project, my big nose, or my red hair would never be a problem again. The invitation on my desk was back to normal: no movies, no light shows, no nothing. Were the child, lion, and lamb part of the miniature movie? The dreams made me feel great, but I awoke with more questions. The answers, though, would have to wait. It was time for school.

THE JOURNEY BECKONS

The next day, I couldn't concentrate at school. Rather than conjugate verbs and struggle with algebra, I pondered the invitation and the dreams. It seemed I couldn't resist their pull, drawn like a magnet to metal. My thoughts drifted from the child, lion, and lamb to the mountain alive with colors, to the crowning jewel of a castle. I wanted to be there, in *that* world.

"Alli?" Ms. Prickle croaked my name. "Alli!" she said more sharply, demanding my attention this time.

"Hmm? Yes, um, Ms. Prickle? I'm…uh sorry, Ma'am. What did you say?"

"Alli, will you repeat my instructions for the class regarding the writing assignment?"

Embarrassed, I turned ten shades of red (what, with my red hair and all, was *never* a good look). I stuttered nervously, "Uh…uh…uh…I'm sorry, Ma'am. I…I can't."

"Well, then," Ms. Prickle said icily, "maybe you can share with everyone what's more important than paying attention in my class?"

Oh, man! The *one* time I daydreamed. The *one* time, and I got caught. What's up with that?

"I'm sorry, Ma'am." I hung my head in shame.

"Well, don't let it happen again, Miss Alli!"

"Yes, Ma'am," I replied sheepishly.

Ms. Prickle cured me of daydreaming for the rest of the day. As the stinging embarrassment was fresh on my mind, I vowed to *never* daydream in class again. I shrunk further into my seat, trying to disappear. My peers made me uncomfortable, and everyone was staring at me now. Maybe that's why I enjoyed my dream world so much. I didn't have to interact with anybody else. I could just be a spectator and watch things happen in my dreams. Invisible was comfortable for me. Until the run-in with Ms. Prickle, I had managed to lay low at school; but for a few miserable moments, that was out the window. With any luck, my classmates would, once again, forget I ever existed. I thought, *Remember how you survived so far and don't forget. Pay attention! Do your work! Keep to yourself! Obey the rules!* No matter how much the dreams and invitation pulled on my thoughts, I had to resist. I had to focus…at least until I got home from school. For now, I needed to get to geography class, so I shuffled through the hallway with my head down, making sure everyone left me alone.

Later that night, Mom asked, "Alli, can we have a chat?"

Oh no! Can this day get any worse? Now, what does she

want? I thought, exasperated. I wanted to disappear into my room, work on my science project, and forget about the humiliation of the day. But no such luck!

I approached her and sighed, "You wanted to talk to me?"

Mom looked at me, smiling tenderly, "Alli, I've been wondering what you think about your invitation?"

"Oh, um, I don't know. Honestly, Mom, I'm trying to figure it out." I didn't want to talk about it, not yet. Could she just leave me alone!

"Okay, honey. But remember, you have three days to decide. Since this is the third day, I was curious what you had chosen."

"Umm...uh...well...really...ugh. I haven't decided," I waffled.

"All right, dearest. No worries. I wanted to check on my girl's heart and let you know I'm here for you." Mom continued, "I remember things were a bit strange for me after I received my invitation. If you need me, I'm here. Okay?"

"Yeah, okay," I said, shrugging my shoulders.

I hurried down the hall to escape my mom's questions. I loved my mom. She was great and all, but I just wanted to be left alone. When I was worried or upset, I was never the kind of kid who talked about feelings. Yuck! I preferred to work it out alone. I'd think about whatever was bothering me, and after some time passed, it usually got better. And if thinking about it on my own didn't work, I would ignore it until it went away. If I ignored anything long enough, it would go away…or so I thought.

In my room, I looked at the invitation just staring back at me. I wished I hadn't received the invitation in the first place. Everything turned upside down since its arrival. I disliked even the littlest disturbance of my routine, and this went way beyond a little disturbance. The whole situation was bizarre. Had I imagined the whole thing? No. I couldn't deny the glaring evidence sitting on my desk, the invitation. I couldn't handle thinking about it anymore. I would decide what to do later. Overwhelmed, I sighed and escaped into my homework.

A KNIGHT IN THE NIGHT

I must have fallen asleep doing my homework because I awoke to a knock on my door. I was still at my desk; my head was on my arm, and I was drooling. I heard the knock again and waited for a sliver of hallway light to fill my room as Mom opened the door, but nothing happened. Who was knocking? Mom always opened the door after she knocked. Was the door locked? Hazy with sleep, I got up from my desk and stumbled to the door. Nope, not locked. What the heck was going on?

Groggily, I opened the door and couldn't believe my eyes. Standing in front of me was a complete stranger, but that wasn't all: he was dressed like a knight. *A knight in King Arthur's court!* Startled, I blinked several times, expecting him to disappear; however, he stood there in a full suit of armor. Thankfully, his face shield was raised. At least, I could see he had a face. A faceless knight would have really freaked me out!

"By order of His Most Royal Highness, the King. I have been dispatched to your door, Mistress, for the summons that was sent. The King has sent me to receive your reply. Do you accept or reject His Most Magnificent Royal Highness?"

What was happening? Was I still dreaming? I pinched myself. Ouch! Nope, not dreaming.

"I...umm?" I stuttered. "Accept or reject? I...I...I... don't...know. Uh, what are you talking about?"

Looking distressed, he replied, "Did you not receive His Most High, Most Royal, Most Majestic, Most Magnificent, Great One's invitation?"

Invitation? Like a bolt of lightning, it hit me...*the invitation*! My hand smacked my forehead as it dawned on me. *He* was my escort to the banquet. Oh no! Was it already midnight? I had put off the decision till the last minute. Dumbly, I shook my head and tried to clear the cobwebs. What was I going to tell this strange man...I mean knight, or messenger, or escort, or whatever he was? He stood at my door, waiting for an answer.

"But, but, but I'm na...not ready!" I stuttered.

"Pardon me, Mistress. What do you mean you're not ready? Didn't you know I would call on you?"

"Umm...noooo," I stammered again. "Na, na...not really."

"I can extend my wait by five minutes, but no more, Mistress. You are not the only invitee. Please decide quickly. The invitation must be returned to the King," he leaned in for emphasis, "*with* or without you."

Wow! I started to panic. What was I going to do? Was any of this actually real? Suddenly, the calm from my dreams filled me again. In a rush, I remembered everything that had happened since the invitation's arrival. What did I have to lose anyway? I wanted more out of life. My heart longed for something more: friends, family, not being alone all the time.

"Yes!" I blurted out. "I…I will go! Let me get my things."

"You won't need anything," my escort announced. "The King supplies all your needs. All that is needed…is you," he said with a satisfied smile.

"All of my needs?" I asked.

"Yes, *all*," he stressed.

What had I gotten myself into? I was puzzled.

"You must trust the goodness of the King. He is good, Mistress. You will discover it for yourself, in time. He can be mysterious, but you will realize His goodness."

"Oh, okay, I guess I'm ready." I hurriedly grabbed my invitation, slid on my slippers, and followed him out of my room.

As we walked down the hall, I began my "observe and be quiet" mode. I would just be quiet and take it all in. At the end of the hallway, I started to turn left; however, my escort went straight…straight through the wall of my house. *Whaaat? What just happened?* Before I could figure it out, he reached back, grabbed my hand, and the wall disappeared.

Unexpectedly, we were on the path from my dreams, but this time it was different. I felt wide awake and very much alive; the whole scene felt incredibly real. We entered a world bright and beautiful; gone was the nighttime. My escort no longer held my hand and set a very rapid pace in front of me. How would I keep up with him? I was still in my slippers…Or was I? I looked down at my feet and saw the biggest hiking boots I'd ever seen. These were *not* my slippers. The boots came up past my ankle by at least three inches and were a bit ugly, I might add. They looked quite bulky, but they didn't feel heavy or clunky. Really, they were the most comfortable shoes I had ever worn. I couldn't help but notice they added a nice little bounce to each step. Above the boots were very comfortable jeans; my shirt was a deep purple with silver trim. A light jacket finished the ensemble. What a surprise! I guess he meant it when he said all my needs would be met. Who knew?

Rapidly, the new world around me came to life. A breathtaking beautiful sunrise filled the sky with pink, magenta, orange, blue, and purple splendor. How was there a sunrise in full daylight? Birds were in flight, and their songs burst forth everywhere. The new world was obviously different from the world I had just left. While I relished my beautiful, new surroundings, a sense of dread came over me, and a chill rolled down my spine. My guide stopped and abruptly pulled his shield and sword out of nowhere. Where did they come from? I hadn't even finished my thought when he spoke.

"Come quickly, Mistress. Come here, under my protection." Dismayed and fearful, I ran close to him.

He looked around and boldly demanded, "All right, Snake, where are you? I know you're here! Show yourself now, in the name of the King!"

I heard a hissing snake-like voice, "Oh, Perceptive One. Who isss thisss with you now? Did you bring me another deliciousss morsssel for my lair?"

"Be gone with you! You have no place here! In the name of the King, remove yourself, or I will cut off your head!"

The snake started hissing louder, "Yesss, I will go, sssss, but I'll be back. You know thisss one isss mine. Ssshe hasn't gotten to the sssacred land yet. Ssshe belongs to me. Just becaussse your King isss trying to take what isss mine doesn't mean I'm going to let you have her. Come here, little one, sssss...Don't believe thisss ugly knight," he soothed. "He isss the one who isss going to hurt you, not me."

Somehow, his voice became soothing and rhythmic. I felt drawn to the snake's voice and lulled to sleep. I moved away from my escort, walking toward the voice. Stepping off the path, I was light-headed and drowsy, drifting and drifting. As my eyes closed, I heard my escort's call echoing in the distance.

"Mistress! Mistress! Come back. You've gotten off the path. Don't believe his lies!" Then he exclaimed to the snake, "Serpent! Be gone, now, by the authority in the name of the King of the Most High Realm."

Immediately, I snapped awake. My head had almost nodded to my chest, and I was about to fall over. "Wha...

Wha…What was that?" I stammered.

My escort replied, "That, my dear, was the darkest foe of the realm. The serpent realized I was taking you to the castle of the Great King. He knew if you entered into the kingdom, the King would sever his authority over your life."

"Authority over my life? I don't understand."

"Mistress, I'm sorry. These things are not for me to explain. Your teacher will soon be here to instruct you on all of this."

He hurried me along, "Keep moving; it's not safe here. There's a spot, not much further, where we can stop for breakfast."

Once again, my escort traveled at a brisk pace; but after the whole snake thing and all, I was very motivated to keep up. I was not a scaredy-cat or anything, but I didn't like conflict. I went out of my way to avoid it at all costs. If I had known something like the snake would happen, I wouldn't have come. I was so rattled I wondered if it was too late to turn back.

I barely finished my thought when I heard a soft whisper, "It will be okay. I am here with you."

Who said that? Familiar waves of calm washed over me. I felt happy. I didn't understand any of the things that were happening. But I liked the feelings I had experienced since the invitation arrived. Oh no! The invitation. I hoped I hadn't dropped it along the way.

My escort interrupted my thoughts; he stopped, turned around, and looked at me. He declared, "You didn't lose your invitation. It's right there, in your pack."

"In my pack? I don't have a pack!" I exclaimed.

How in the world did he know what I was thinking?

"Now you do!" he said excitedly. "Remember I told you our good King will supply all your needs." And with that, he handed me the most beautiful backpack. And yes, my invitation was inside.

"You are going to receive treasures along your journey. You will need this pack to keep them close to you. These gifts will enable you to stay true to the King."

This journey sounded much harder than I expected. Had I made the right choice to follow this knight? What had I gotten myself into? I thought we would take a quiet walk on a nice trail to a beautiful castle. As soon as doubt-filled thoughts rushed in, waves of calm crowded them out and restored my sense of well-being. Whew! I relaxed and already felt more confident. *You can do this! You can do this!* I coached myself. I remembered the invitation's bold promise to be the "greatest adventure of all!" One thing was for sure: the trip would not be a quiet walk on a nice little trail. As I settled into that thought, I excitedly looked ahead.

Where was the rest stop? I was starving.

RESPITE AND REST

Thankfully, we didn't have to travel much further before we stopped for breakfast. My escort led me to a beautiful spot, an oasis, really. We walked a few steps off the main path and headed toward a clearing. A heavy canopy of trees protected us from the sun, while colorful flowers adorned the edges of the cobbled path. The lush grass was sprinkled with blooming wildflowers. What a beautiful place for breakfast! Slowly, the adventures of the morning melted away.

As we drew closer to the clearing, I saw a crystal blue pond in the center. The water was clear enough to see all the way to the bottom. The pond must be fed by an underground stream, as I could see ripples flowing through the water. Large ornate benches lined the pond, much bigger and grander than the ones back home. Unlike the usual boring ivy, the benches had wrought ironwork featured in the center of their backs, which was fascinating. The first bench had a large lion's head, while the opposite bench had a large lamb's head. Both centerpieces were highlighted with swirls of angels and fairies. The clearing wasn't like any other place I'd ever seen. For sure, this was a different world.

A grand pavilion covered in the most massive grapevines bursting with the largest, ripest grapes was near the pond. They looked deliciously sweet, and I was so hungry. Without a thought, I plucked a bunch of grapes and plopped one in my mouth. Mmmmm. So good. Uh-oh! Was I allowed to do that? Guiltily, I glanced at my escort. He looked back at me and laughed.

He smiled and said, "Yes, Mistress! Don't worry. Most everyone has the same reaction when they see the fruit here. The fruit of the kingdom of the Great King *is* irresistible. Go on." He reassured me, "It is okay to enjoy the fruits. I warn you, though, the fruit on these vines is quite filling: just a few pieces may fill you up for the day. Save some room for the breakfast the King's servants are preparing."

"Breakfast the King's servants are preparing?" I echoed.

"Yes, the King is aware of you and your journey. He is such a good King. He would never invite you to His home without making provisions for you along the way. Remember? All your needs will be met. This only happens by the goodness of the Great King."

Around a mouth full of the most delicious grapes, I mumbled, "Thank you."

Despite my guide's warning, I kept stuffing my mouth with grapes. In my love of food, grapes have always been one of my favorites. The juicy, perfectly ripened fruit was sweet as honeysuckle. But ten times more delicious than any I'd had.

From the corner of my eye, I saw a flurry of activity headed toward me. A whole team of people, probably the King's servants, appeared with food-filled platters. Wonderful smells filled the air. *I must be dreaming!* I thought. Food didn't normally smell this delicious.

"Welcome, Mistress! Hello! Welcome!" in chorus, the servants greeted me as they curtsied and smiled. They carefully set the table, positioned the food, and poured the beverages within moments. Everyone moved in unison. Quietly, in awe and disbelief, I watched their well-synchronized dance.

My escort smiled, "Things are run very differently around here. The King's realm is most efficient, well-oiled, and precisely set. We are like the famed Swiss watch admired by your world for its precision. Our King is very precise."

"Oh," I responded and shrank back.

Excellence and precision? Hmmm...I was very aware I lacked those traits. I was many things, but "precise" and "excellent" weren't on the list. All my life, I avoided being too good or too bad at anything. Life seemed to revolve around people who were really good or bad at things, but anyone in the middle got overlooked. I called the people in the middle "the hidden ones" because no one noticed them. So, I figured if I could stay in the middle and not make waves, no one would notice me...and that's how I liked it.

Unexpectedly, I heard a voice coming from somewhere

near my waist. "Why here, in the King's realm, nothing is hidden from the Great King. You see, He loves and cares for all who travel here. No one, I tell you, no one, goes unnoticed."

Who said that? I looked down and was startled to see a lamb. *A lamb!* He just stood there as easy as you please. I thought, *Are talking animals normal here? What in the world? Is he the lamb from my dream? The one with the boy and the lion?*

"Right you are, Mistress. I am the lamb you saw with the child on the path. Wasn't he a delight? The boy, I mean. I truly liked the song he sang the night you saw us."

Dumbfounded, I stood there with my mouth agape.

"It's okay, Mistress," my guide offered. "Nothing is what you're used to. And no, this is *not* a dream! This is very real...more real than anything in your world."

When I looked up, the King's servants were patiently waiting to seat and serve us.

"Shall we?" My guide extended his arm and escorted me to my seat on the right of the table head. Then he took the seat across from me. Much to my surprise, the lamb sat in a kingly chair at the head of the table. *He must be the guest of honor*, I guessed. Whoa! All of this was totally different than home. Animals were never allowed in the dining room, let alone the head of the table. Lambs? There was no way! I'd heard stories about old ladies letting cats on the table or dogs sitting under it, begging...but a lamb at the *head* of the table? Just the thought stunned me, keeping my mouth shut even more.

"My favorites are the crêpes. They are like angel food, light as a feather," the lamb leaned over and secretly divulged.

I stared at the table, covered with platters of food from end to end. I had never seen a feast like this. Apparently, my host, the lamb, saw the look of wonder on my face.

He chuckled. "Don't be dismayed. You don't have to eat all this by yourself. This is our welcome feast prepared for all our travelers to show them how very special they are to us. We know your journey will be difficult at times. We prepared this feast to sustain you." The lamb continued, "From time to time, you may need to remember this place. When you do, you will know you are welcomed and wanted here. We want you to discover this truth. Even if everything around tells you something different, try and remember it is true."

Next, children and a few grown-ups joined us: a woodsman, a peasant woman, a scullery maid, and a few others. Animals of every kind joined us also; to my relief, not all the animals sat with us. But everyone seemed to have a place to enjoy the feast.

While looking around at the guests, I spotted a horse off in the distance. How had I missed him earlier? Before I could give it much thought, the lamb stood upright on his chair and called everyone to attention. It was a good thing he had such a kingly chair; otherwise, it might've toppled over.

The lamb declared:

"Welcome one; welcome all,

Welcome to our welcome call.

Today Alli has responded to our invitation.

As she begins her journey through the dark

And through the light to our kingdom hall,

We are gathered here to cheer her on!

So, in the name of our Great King,

We thank Him and thank you all,

For joining us at this welcome call."

As soon as the lamb sat down, everyone passed around the food platters and filled their plates. Meanwhile, on my left, amid the passing platters, the loveliest voice grabbed my attention.

"Would you care for some Stellar Ice?"

"Stellar Ice?" I queried and turned toward the speaker. Silenced in awe once again, I saw the loveliest creature: a fairy maiden. Her hair and dress radiated beauty. Her white, flowy dress was covered in a wispy sheath of light and color that ebbed and flowed like the invitation. As she moved, colors splashed on the table, on me, and on the food. *Is she a fairy?* I wondered to myself. *Where are her wings?* My eyes snuck a glance of her back. *Yep, there they are, folded neatly behind her in the chair...wings.* Like everything in this world, she was fairylike yet different from anything I had ever seen or even imagined.

Our host, the lamb, leaned over to me and said, "Eat up, little one. You'll be leaving soon."

Laughter and joy surrounded me. The talking sounded like a rhythmic song, getting softer and louder, creating a sweet harmony. It was awesome! I sat silently in my usual posture of "quiet observer." Although I was fascinated by everything, I was nervously looking around. I didn't know who or what I'd see next. Maybe there was a toad king at the other end of the table. I chuckled to myself.

Despite all the action during the banquet, I managed to fill my plate. My love for food would not let me down! I could eat no matter what was happening. The food was amazing! Don't get me wrong: my mom was an awesome cook, but she never made food quite like this. For lack of a better word, the banquet food simply tasted more...*alive*. The bursting flavors in my mouth made my tongue do a happy dance. The feast was like Easter, my birthday, and Christmas all at once. It was that good!

Although the lamb said we had to go soon, I noted he spoke with *every* guest. He took time for everyone. He stared intently at them with his piercing blue eyes. As I observed the look of joy and love on their faces, it seemed they felt like he loved them best. How did he do that? As the banquet ended, the guests filed out to begin their day.

The lamb made sure to leave them with a kind word, "We loved having you. Please come again soon. You know it wouldn't be the same without you."

The fairy maiden seated next to me laughed as she watched me watching the lamb. Her laughter was lilting and beautiful, tinkling on the air as it floated over me. Suddenly it hit my insides all at once. I didn't see it coming and burst out laughing! Full-on belly laughing. I laughed so hard that everyone stopped and stared at me. In an instant, they were laughing too. Laughter hit some folks so hard they fell to the ground and rolled around. Outrageous, uproarious laughter broke out everywhere. I would have fallen out of my chair, but it was pushed close to the table.

My escort came up behind me and asked, "Mistress, may I assist you?"

With one stealth move, he pulled out my chair and stood me up. Carefully, he assisted my bent-over form to a grassy area away from the table. I gladly surrendered to the ground and laughed even harder. Before I knew it, all the remaining guests were beside me laughing. I looked up and saw the fairy floating near us. She touched us with some sort of scepter extended from her hand. As the colors from her sparkling dress danced and splashed around, mixing with the iridescent swirls of light from her wand, the laughter rolled over us.

A small child with playful sparkles in his eyes locked glances with me. As we stared at each other, giggles and more giggles came rolling out of us. The laughter continued to move and reignite throughout the pavilion. Simple glances and shared looks were all it took to restart the laughter. No matter beast or man, if our eyes met, we burst into laughter again and again. I didn't want it to end; I'd never had that much fun...like ever.

But alas, the journey had to continue. Slowly we picked ourselves up, made our way to the end of the park, and gathered by the crystal blue pond. Everyone said goodbye to me and wished me well. They all hugged me and told me they would keep me in their thoughts and prayers, "Rest assured, we'll meet again at the Great Banquet of the King!" Their hugs felt like my mom's hugs…warm, comforting. I didn't realize it until much later, but I wasn't even stiff or uncomfortable. I guess I was still feeling the effects of my new fairy friend.

TRAVELING COMPANIONS

After most of the guests left, I noticed the lamb and fairy remained. Had they stayed to speak with my guide? I waited while they chatted. Enthralled by the beautiful scenery, my eyes wandered across the trees and hills, from the birds to the beautiful flowers. I took it all in, and then I saw him. Oh, there he was…the most remarkable horse ever! Stately and tall, his pure white mane and tail waved in the gentle breeze. Even though he was far away, his eyes shone like fire. His exquisite beauty drew me. I had to get a better look at him. I just had to!

I felt the fairy's eyes on me and darted a nervous but excited glance in her direction.

"Would you like to pet him?" she asked.

I nodded, thrilled. "Would I? Yes!" I would…more than anything.

"Go ahead," she encouraged.

My heart raced. I wanted to run straight for him, but the butterflies in my stomach held me back. I gingerly

53

made my way through the grassy meadow to reach him. He quietly ate his breakfast and lightly pawed the ground. As the gap between us narrowed, my excitement turned to sheer panic. At first, I didn't think he noticed me, which was okay because I was so nervous I could barely breathe. After a few moments, he gently snorted and nodded in my direction. It was a gentle nod, but I'm pretty sure it was horsespeak for "hello." A smile crept across my face, and I exhaled a quiet sigh of relief. As quickly as he noticed me, he turned his attention back to his bin of food. Mesmerized by his magnificence, I watched him eat his simple breakfast of oats and hay. He lapped up water from a rather interesting bowl. The water flowed and bubbled like a fountain fed by an underground spring. Curiously, no matter how much it bubbled, it never overflowed. How could that be? Before I could figure it out, he interrupted me with a sudden snort.

"Hey there, boy," I mustered up the courage to say.

Unable to stop myself, I saw my hand move gently toward his nose. *What are you doing? Be careful!* I screamed to myself. I was afraid. Forcing myself to take a deep breath, I let it out slowly to calm my nerves. Somehow, I knew it would be okay. Just as my hand reached his muzzle, he looked at me. In that instant, we locked eyes for the first time. What I experienced next was barely describable. His white mane seemed alive like fire, blowing and waving rhythmically in the wind. His eyes were deep pools of icy blue, a stark contrast to his otherwise white face. His gaze penetrated the very depths of me as if he saw right through me. Startled by the power and presence of his gaze, I stumbled backward slightly, scared and exhilarated at the same time.

"In our world, creatures understand much more than they do in your world. You will notice things are very different here than what you are used to," the fairy spoke.

I spun around to discover that my guide and the fairy had joined me on the hill. I was so fascinated by the horse I didn't hear them approach.

She encouraged me gently, "Go ahead; you may continue to pet him."

I nodded and carefully reached back to pat his head. Quietly, I marveled. After a few more pats, I backed away and waited for my next instruction.

"If you're ready, Mistress, we will go. We still have a long road ahead of us." My guide told me, "A lady-in-waiting has brought us provisions of food and fresh water from the living stream. We must go."

Then the lamb walked over to me...upright, which, if I might add, still took a bit of getting used to. I thought, *He must be a close friend of the King.*

"May I give you a gift, Mistress?" he asked excitedly.

"Su...Su...Sure," I stuttered, nervous at the very idea of receiving a gift from him.

The next thing I knew, the lamb bowed his curly, fleecy head, and a glimmering cloud of gold emanated from him. The gold aura passed from him to me: enveloping, surrounding, and then passing through me. Somehow, I felt the beauty of the gold sparkling inside me. The aura left a rich deposit of liquid gold, which warmed me on the inside. After a few moments, the glimmering cloud of gold disappeared. I realized there was something very special about this lamb...something *very, very* special.

Was the gold aura the gift? Just then, the lamb handed me a small, silver trumpet. The ancient trumpet was etched with beautiful scrollwork. On one side was the head of a mighty lion, while on the other side was a lamb's head, much like the ironwork on the park benches. Was the lamb on the trumpet the same lamb standing in front of me?

"Blow this trumpet whenever you need aid, and it will come to you," the lamb instructed, his piercing blue eyes sharp with intensity. "This is the first of the treasures you will receive on your journey. Thank you so much for coming, Alli. We are so delighted you accepted our invitation." Then with a smile and a wink, he added, "The feast just would not be the same without you."

Why did I feel so loved by this furry little creature? Completely loved. Could I be a favorite too? This was my first time feeling like a favorite from someone I had just met...and I liked it. Gratitude filled my heart for everything that happened in this place of rest and refreshment.

"Thank you very much," I said shyly. Bowing clumsily, I turned to place the trumpet in my backpack. Oh no! I laid my backpack down at the park. Before my next panicked thought could arise, I saw my backpack lying neatly on the ground beside me. Who put that there? I carefully placed my beautiful, new treasure in the bag.

"Are you ready, Mistress?" my guide asked.

"Yes," I nodded and followed him to the path.

After several minutes of quietly strolling down the road, I heard a noise behind us and looked over my shoulder. We were not alone. The beautiful white horse trotted alongside the gliding fairy. My escort and I slowed down so they could catch up to us.

When they joined us, the fairy said sweetly, "I'm so excited to be here with you. I have waited for this special day for a very long time."

"Really?" I asked, bewildered anyone was excited to spend time with me...especially a mystical creature like her.

"May we join you on your journey for a bit?"

"Yes! Of course!" I blurted out, which wasn't like me, but I knew she had so many important things to do, yet she wanted to hang out with me!

Knowingly, she looked at me and said, "Alli, dear girl, you are very important to the King. He sent me to be your friend and help you on your journey. The King's only requirement for you is a willing heart. Your acceptance of His invitation showed you have that." I stared intently into her beautiful face as she spoke. It was unreal being with a fairy; I was hanging on to every word.

"If you let me love you, I will always be right here." She motioned toward my chest. "There may be times when you cannot see me, but I will always be with you. You will find me here, in your heart."

I didn't understand what she meant. *How can she be in my heart? How can she be with me when I cannot see her?*

She saw my confusion and responded, "Oh, Alli, there are some things you can't figure out with your keen intellect. Some things you can only understand with your heart and your spirit. I am here to teach you the way of the King."

She reached out her delicate hand and waved it lightly over my head. As her hand passed over my head, a wave of peace washed through me. Although I'd felt the peace before, this time was different. I felt love seeping in like a gentle rain, and it smelled like the sweetest roses in a warm summer breeze. In that moment, I figured it all out. Okay, maybe I didn't figure it *all* out; but I did figure out something important. *She* was the teacher my guide told me about. She would help me understand this strange, new world.

"There," she said, satisfied. "That is better!" She smiled and turned back to the path. Stunned and awestruck, I stood there and watched the horse, the guide, and the fairy continue down the path. I was a bit dazed.

"Alli?" the fairy called to me, "are you coming, dear?"

"Oh, yeah!" I exclaimed and ran to catch up with them.

As I rejoined our little group, I recognized the new surroundings on the path. Was this the place where I saw the lion, the lamb, and the child in my dream? How could that be possible—that place was in a dream? I remembered my mom told me the adventure would happen when I slept.

Was everything a dream? Ever since I'd gotten here, the guide and the fairy kept assuring me their world was more real than my own. Things were getting harder to grasp, but now wasn't the time to sort it all out. We had to keep going, so I pushed my questions aside and returned to my true nature...observer mode. I would watch, wait, and see what happened next.

The fairy asked, "Alli, would you like to know your companions' names?"

"Yes, please," I replied eagerly.

She lifted her hand, pointed toward the horse, and said, "This is Swift. And this is Rhey"; she shifted my attention to my guide. He flashed me a kind smile, which I quickly returned. Lastly, with a beautiful, graceful bow, the fairy said, "My name is Saraiyah." Her warm smile was so welcoming I felt like she really was glad to be with me.

"Saraiyah," I repeated in a whisper. What a perfect name for such an ethereal creature!

LEARNING IN A NEW LAND

"Pardon me," I asked. "How should I address you? Should I call you Ma'am or Miss or Your Most High Fairyness?"

Saraiyah's tinkling laughter filled the air. "Just call me Ima."

"Ima? I thought your name was Saraiyah."

"Yes," she replied. "Saraiyah is the name most people know, but Ima is a special name. Ima is the name I share with the ones I am helping on their way to the King's castle. You see, Alli, 'Ima' means 'mother.' In the King's realm, I will be like a mother to you and more." Her eyes shined as she smiled. "Just like you hear your conscience, I will speak to you inside. I will comfort you and love you unconditionally. At times, I will even correct you. In all these ways, I will enable you to arrive safely to the realm of the King."

After we walked on for a bit, Saraiyah continued, "I will teach you many things, but some things will be caught rather than taught. This learning will happen, with your great ability to observe." She was smiling, but then her eyes narrowed, and she stared at me. "Of the many things you will learn, never forget: you must *never* leave the path, which is the way of the King. As you journey to the King's realm, the serpent may tempt you to go off the path. Or convince you to do it on your own. You mustn't. You must never leave the path by yourself," she said unusually sternly.

Uneasy referring to anyone else as a mom, I stuttered, "Im...Im...Ima...but I thought we were already in the realm of the King?"

Before Saraiyah could answer, Rhey directed us to a much-needed rest area beside the path. I snacked on some grapes while Saraiyah continued my lesson. "We are on the borders of the King's realm. Long ago, our Great King gave this beautiful land to a steward. The King raised him like His own son. He placed him here to learn how to be a ruler. Our Great King was far too wise to give His entire kingdom to an untried steward. The King visited the steward daily, walking and talking with him in a beautiful garden. The steward's life was perfect until one day the serpent—" she paused and knowingly glanced my way. "I believe you've met him already."

"Uh-huh," I mumbled nervously.

"Well, one day, the serpent tricked the steward into believing a bunch of lies. The greatest lie claimed the King didn't truly love him. Even though the King treated the steward like a son, the steward believed the snake's lies instead.

"The conversation went a bit like this:

"'The King is just usssing you.' The snake lisped, 'He doesn't actually love you. He sssent you here to keep you from being great. You know you are not Hisss son. The King only pretendsss He wants you to be in Hisss family, but He'sss just using you. He wantsss you to increase Hisss kingdom with all your hard work, and then He'sss going to take the kingdom back and leave you forever.'"

I listened, enthralled. What a story!

"The serpent was cunning and lured the steward into a web of lies, which entangled him and stole his identity, his true purpose. You see, Alli," Saraiyah sighed sadly, "Our King had planned for His beloved steward to be regent with the crown prince as an adopted brother. The King was training the steward to co-rule and co-reign with His one true son. He loved the steward very, very much, but the serpent tricked the steward into believing otherwise."

"How did the serpent trick the steward?" I asked.

"Well, you see, the snake used to have legs, just like the man. They stood face-to-face while he told the steward lies. The latter made the mistake of listening to the serpent and staring into his eyes. As he spoke, the serpent released a poisonous mist, which engulfed the steward and clouded his mind. The confused steward believed the serpent's lies and surrendered his soul."

"His soul?" I asked worriedly.

"Yes, child," she explained, "whenever you believe in something, you give your heart to it. When you give your heart to it, you give your soul to it as well. By believing the snake, he closed his heart to the King and opened it to the serpent."

"What happened to the steward?" I asked.

"Sadly," Saraiyah answered, "the steward paid a high price for listening to the serpent. His choices brought darkness upon himself and his family. Because of this, the King had to banish him to The Void, the empty, desolate land with thorns and thistles. But our King never abandoned him. He kept watch over the steward and his children. He even paid the blood price so he could return. Our King longed for the day the steward would want to come back to his real home. Relying solely on the abundance of the King's mercies, the steward made his home in The Void. He worked incredibly hard there and faced many challenges."

How sad for him. The steward lost everything, I thought.

"Yes, it was sad," Saraiyah replied.

Secretly, I wiped a tear from my eye. Had she read my mind? I shot her a surprised glance.

Saraiyah smiled and said, "Miss Alli, I know a little bit about your thoughts. You're not the first person I've helped along this journey. I am much older than I appear. I've been doing this for a very long time."

"How long?" I asked.

"Oh my!" she replied whimsically, "Since time before

time." She winked and left it at that!

Since before time? How old could she be anyway? Didn't she ever age? She was so beautiful. I looked closely at her lovely face. Her skin was a kaleidoscope of colors, changing with every swirl of light, radiating from her in every direction. She was alive with color and the ethnic colors of all people. A perfect cupid's bow framed her full red lips, while her cheeks were the shade of rose petals. A perfectly shaped nose sat nicely in the frame of her face. Her eyes, though, were her most beautiful feature, unlike anything on earth. They were deep pools of violet, filled with stunning swirls of sapphire blue and flashes of white light. They were powerful and peaceful, all at the same time. They were amazing. *She* was amazing!

Saraiyah's hair shone as beautifully as her face. Unlike my unruly red mop, her hair was a pretty platinum color, piled high atop her head in an intricate up-do. A delicate tiara encircled her beautiful soft curls. Colors of the rainbow constantly flickered and swirled around her. She sparkled all over and shined like a star. It was difficult to stare at her very long because she radiated a piercing light like the brightest sun. She was the most beautiful being I had ever seen, and she wanted to be with *me*!

Saraiyah kindly smiled as if she knew my thoughts again.

"Shall we continue our journey?"

Ahead of us, I watched Swift and Rhey. They walked together as if they'd been best friends forever. Saraiyah caught my hand and quietly walked beside me. Her nearness felt so familiar. Had it been Saraiyah, in my dreams, walking beside me behind the bushes? Had she always been there? That's when I knew I would never be alone again. I would have my own personal fairy; how cool is that! This beautiful being beside me was my companion and would be with me one way or another...always. While we walked, I sensed she wasn't just holding my hand but also my heart. It almost took my breath away. I'd placed walls around my heart to feel safer by keeping other people out. I could feel the fortress around my heart crumbling under the weight of her hand. Saraiyah's presence was tearing down the walls. She tenderly smiled and released my hand. "Daughter, the Great King equipped me to fill your heart with a taste of His love. We want you to know how very much you are loved and wanted. And you know what? You are lovable to us."

"Lovable?"

How is this possible? They don't even know me.

Saraiyah smiled. "You will understand more as time passes, but for now, please know: you being here is not an accident. The Great King knows all things and understands your heart better than you do. You are handpicked and invited to come on this journey. He wants to show you all that's hidden inside of you. While here, you will discover the Great King's love for you, and it's in His love that you will find your true self. You see, the steward is not the only beloved child who believed the lies of the serpent! That dragon!" she spoke passionately, "That father of lies has whispered into the hearts and minds of the King's children since the world began."

Maybe it was the astonished look on my face or her own resolve, but she quickly said, "Okay, that is enough for today. The night is coming, and we need to find a place to rest. You have had a big day, dear Alli. You need your sleep."

DESERT OASIS

Tired? Boy, wasn't that the truth! What a day! I was exhausted. Weariness set in, and I didn't care where I slept. A bed of leaves and a rock for a pillow looked good to me at that moment. As we plodded along, I reviewed the day that started at midnight. No wonder I was so tired! It felt like we squeezed several days into one. So much happened in one day.

After what seemed like forever, Rhey directed us toward a thickly forested area; ducking down, we climbed into the thicket. My mind raced for a few moments, *What about Swift? Oh no, how will he make it through the thicket?* I shot a brief glance over my shoulder to check on him. There he was, my gallant Swift, on his horsey knees close behind me. How was he doing that? He looked so funny: legs tucked in as tight as could be. I giggled to myself.

As we pushed through, the scenery around us changed dramatically. What had been an almost impassable thicket just moments ago was now a beautiful oasis. The path's brambly brush transformed into thick, lush grass.

Overgrown bushes gave way to well-manicured flowering bushes, and wild twisted trees became stately towering oaks. I couldn't believe my eyes. Where had the oasis come from?

While Swift trotted to a patch of young grass beside the quiet stream, I stood and waited to see where I would sleep. Despite the nice surroundings, I couldn't think of anything *but* sleep. Just as I yawned again, I noticed Rhey pulled out a very small tent. He quickly put it up and opened the flap for me to enter. "Come, Mistress," he said. I bent down and climbed inside. Instantly, my sleep-filled eyes opened wide with amazement. The tiny two-person tent had become as large as a circus tent! A wall of opaque white curtains hung as a divider on my right. They appeared light and airy, but I couldn't see through them. Rhey gently directed me toward the curtains and nodded his head to go in.

I opened the curtains, and everything in the tent was a feast for the eyes, full of textures and colors, fine threads, and embroidery. Vivid oranges, teals, golds, and reds splashed on the bed, covered in a cloud of blankets and a rainbow of pillows. My intent gaze spotted a tray of food that was as beautiful as the room. There were grapes from my welcome feast, but there were more: yummy-looking cheeses, bright-colored fruits, strange-looking bread, and a small luminescent drink adorned the engraved silver tray. Moving closer to sample my feast, I couldn't help eyeing the elaborate details of the serving ware. The handle of the delicate glass was a silver-wired holder, which encircled the base and swept up the sides in an intricate pattern of fairies and leaves. Lastly, I noticed dime-sized medallions flanking each side of the cup: the lion and the lamb. I was becoming increasingly familiar with these symbols.

My growling stomach made itself known. Oddly, I wasn't hungry until I saw the feast; the welcome breakfast *had* stuck with me. Things were so different here. As I reached for a delicious snack, I looked for Rhey to make sure this was allowed. I couldn't believe all of this was for me. Rhey was smiling at the entrance of the tent. "Yes, Mistress," he said, "please enjoy some food and rest. Refresh yourself. This is all for you. Goodnight, Miss Alli." And he exited the tent.

Everything looked like a scene out of a beautiful, unexpected dream. Relieved, I sat down on the bed. Wow! It was soft, but I didn't sink into it. It was soft but firm… weird…but good weird. I remembered the time I sat on a waterbed and sunk, hitting the wood underneath. Whose bed was that? Oh yeah! It was Mom's aunt Maggie. She was a hippie who loved her waterbed. I couldn't stand it. Thank goodness this was *not* a waterbed.

Eagerly, I devoured my meal. It was delicious! Just like the grapes from my welcome feast, everything had a bursting-at-the-seams flavor. The bread…well, it looked like bread…but I wasn't sure what it was. It was creamy white and small, thin like a wafer. I decided to take a chance and taste it. The "bread" crunched like a cracker but tasted sweet like honey. Mmmm, strangely enough, after a few nibbles, I was full. There was more to this food than met the eye.

After finishing my yummy "bread," I reached for the

luminescent drink. Little fizzy bubbles lined the glass and danced around like soda. My mom never let me drink much soda, but I guessed she wouldn't mind. After all, there was little chance the glowing concoction was really soda. The luminescent color was strange, but strange was becoming normal. I shrugged and took a nice long sip. Oh! It was sweet and syrupy. Immediately, I felt warm liquid sliding down my throat to my belly. The warmth didn't stop there but seeped through every part of me. Warm sensations shot through my arms and legs to my hands and feet. I had never felt or tasted anything like this. It was sweet and delicious. Fizzy and electric. Warm and comforting.

Moments later, Saraiyah came to tuck me in and say goodnight. She gently tucked the cloud-like covers under my chin and sat beside me. As sleep overtook my eyelids, her face grew fuzzier and fuzzier. She smiled and kissed my cheek, just like my mom does. I missed my mom. And with Saraiyah's kiss, I was asleep.

My mom's eyes sparkled as she grinned at me. She gave me the biggest hug. Was she really standing in front of me? Or am I still dreaming?

"So, tell me *all* about your journey so far. Who did you meet? Was there anyone unusual?" she asked excitedly. Her eyes twinkled as if she already knew some of my answers.

"Oh, Mom, you were there. Don't you remember? You know there are so many magical creatures and strange things there!" I laughed, barely containing my excitement.

"Yes, I know, but everyone's experience is unique. I don't want to presume. Please tell me *everything!*"

We sat in the living room, and I excitedly shared what had happened so far, from walking right through the wall of our house to the path, to sleeping in the opulent tent. She smiled and listened. When I mentioned Saraiyah and the lamb, she nodded as if she knew exactly who I meant. She giggled as I told her about the welcome feast, the delicious food, and especially the fizzy syrup drink. I felt so good, sitting and laughing with my mom. I couldn't remember when we had more fun or felt as close.

After I finished my story, she instructed, "Don't be surprised if you don't see me for a while. The new world may consume you as you get further on the journey. But don't worry," she assured me, "I will be right here when you are finished." Her face grew serious, and her eyes narrowed slightly, "Alli, trust the goodness of the King. Always trust the goodness of the King."

She leaned forward and kissed my cheek. I raised my hand to my face and touched the kiss. I awoke the same way I had fallen asleep...with a kiss.

The talk with my mom must have been a dream because I awoke back in the tent. When I was asleep in the new world, I was awake in my world. When I was sleeping in my world, I was awake in the new world. The lines between the worlds were getting quite blurry. I didn't have long to juggle my concerns: as my eyes opened, I was immediately distracted by Saraiyah. She was shining brightly, much more than I remembered. Was it from the dimness around her in the tent? Nooooo, somehow, she had increased her light. She *was actually* shining more brightly.

"Time to rise and shine, sleepyhead," her voice danced over me. Her eyes sparkled and twinkled. "As you can see," she continued, "I've got my shine on! Come on, Alli. It's time to get up. We have a big day ahead of us."

Yawning, I replied, "Another one?"

"Yes!" she sang, "They're *all* big days, even though it may not seem that way. Every day is a gift. Every day you have choices: light or darkness, joy or sadness. You will discover many truths and mysteries along your journey, but you do not have to figure it all out right now, at least not before the King's croissants. Let's get breakfast."

I didn't know what the King's croissants were, but I sure liked the sound of them. I bounded out of bed and grabbed the robe that appeared at the foot of my bed.

A DUNK IN THE DRINK

Breakfast was over rather quickly, as I devoured the yummy King's croissants. I was ready to start the day, so I walked toward the bushes we entered last night.

Saraiyah called to me, "Alli, it's not quite time to go. We are awaiting the King's messenger." Rhey packed up the tent as quick as a wink and motioned me to join them. Dumbfounded, I stood there and stared at them for several moments.

Saraiyah came and took my hand, "Come, little one." She led me to a bench beside a small brook or spring or whatever it was.

"Look into the water," Saraiyah instructed me, "Tell me what you see."

I looked. I didn't really see anything. Just some water was flowing down over rocks, nothing special. I didn't want to disappoint her, but there wasn't anything. Glancing back at her, I shrugged slightly.

"Look again. Keep looking. Be patient," she encouraged

me.

Then I searched the water again, more intently this time. Suddenly, a giant goldfish's head popped out of the water and spat something out of its mouth. Startled, I jumped back slightly. Once I caught my breath, I leaned closer to check out the fish, and the craziest thing happened... it smiled at me. What? Can fish even smile? As quickly as it appeared, the fish ducked back under the surface and swiftly disappeared.

"Whoa! What the heck was that?" I cried.

"Just the King's messenger," Saraiyah replied casually.

She joined me at the water's edge and bent down to pick up the missive from the fish. It was a small tube of tightly rolled paper. Saraiyah unfolded the message, and much to my surprise, the small scroll unraveled several feet. I glanced at the scroll but couldn't read the ornate script.

"Ah, just as I expected," Saraiyah said. "Soon, we will meet more travelers. The enemy has alerted his cohorts of your arrival. Be aware," she warned. "He is on the prowl. Sometimes, Alli," her eyes held mine, "he comes in a way you least expect him."

On the prowl? What did that mean?

There was no time to figure it out because Saraiyah arose and said, "Well, let us be on our way."

I turned toward the way we came, but Saraiyah stopped me. "Oh no! That way will not do!" she exclaimed and took my hand. She looked me in the eye, "Are you ready? Hold your breath."

In an instant, she jumped right into the water with me in tow. Down, down, down we went. Saraiyah swam so elegantly with her wings. I had no idea fairylike creatures or any creatures, for that matter, could swim with wings. A few moments into our watery journey, I wondered if Rhey and Swift would find us. Looking over my shoulder, I spotted them: Rhey was riding Swift. Swift's long legs "galloped" through the water, bringing them closer and closer to us. Just when I thought I would run out of breath, we popped up into an underwater world. We stood on a small land area, like an island. I could breathe perfectly fine as if we had entered an air bubble in the depths of the ocean. All around me were exciting sea creatures: mermaids, mermen, you name it.

Rhey motioned toward a small boat anchored near the shore of our little "island." He walked toward me and took my hand. He didn't say much as we neared the boat. "In you go, Mistress," he said, breaking the silence.

I started climbing into the boat but paused as I noticed Saraiyah speaking to someone. He looked like a mer-king or someone of great importance, as he wore a gold crown and held a beautiful scepter. He looked and acted like he owned the place! Rhey nudged me into the boat and climbed aboard.

"Wait! What about Saraiyah?" I protested.

"Not to worry, Mistress. No one tells Miss Saraiyah what to do. She will rejoin us on her own accord when she is good and ready," he laughed playfully, "and not a minute before. Now then, let's get on with it! We must go. These merfolk were good enough to offer us an escort. Let us not keep them waiting." And with that, we were off.

"But, but, but, what about Swift?" I stammered.

"It is okay, Milady. Swift will find his way."

Things sure did come and go around here in such peculiar ways. Before I got too lost in my thoughts, the escorting merfolk captured my attention. The mermaids and mermen swam and splashed around us, pushing and pulling our little boat. They danced like they were in a deep-sea ballroom. They reminded me of the dolphins back home. I couldn't help but smile. Oh, wait! What? That one *was* a dolphin! I laughed in delight as it jumped in and out of the water alongside our boat.

The ride was exhilarating, with barely a moment to catch my breath. My eyes danced from one marvelous sight to another. The background flew by as we sped, like ninety miles per hour. I was about to close my eyes and enjoy the wind whipping through my hair, but something caught my eye. I saw it...the waterfall. Oh no! A waterfall? Before doing what I usually did best, panic, the merfolk grabbed our boat and thrust it through the waterfall. We jutted through it so fast we barely got wet. One minute we were heading toward a waterfall, and the next minute we were on the other side. As quickly as our journey began, it came to an end. Our destination, the shoreline, was visible, and much to my surprise, Swift was standing at the water's edge. A beautiful mermaid was feeding him an apple and rubbing his nose. She spotted us and slipped back into the water. Her long flowing hair glimmered in the sunlight, and her beautiful tail briefly shone purple and green under the water. Then, with a keen eye and a cool glide, she disappeared back under the waterfall.

Rhey jumped from the boat and guided it to shore. I hopped out and greeted Swift with a pat on his nose. I looked around and noticed a small village just beyond the shoreline. The grass-roof cottages nestling amongst a forest glen looked sweet and inviting...surprisingly normal for this place. With any luck, this was our destination. A quiet, peaceful village seemed like a great place to rest from our wild adventures.

Rhey interrupted my thoughts. "Coming, Mistress?" he inquired.

"Yes, um, huh?" I replied. "My head is still spinning a bit from the ride." He shrugged gently, took my hand, and we headed toward the village.

I don't think I will ever get used to the wildness of this world, I thought to myself.

THE BOOK

The quaint little village looked like it was fresh out of my childhood books. Small brightly-colored cottages lined the small streets: tidy little houses with tidy little trees on tidy little lawns. The scenery brought a favorite book to mind. Lost in thought, I became aware of someone familiar in the distance. Oh, my goodness! It was Saraiyah. How did she get to the village so quickly? It must have been her fairy wings. She had no problem zipping here, zipping there.

Saraiyah sat with a maiden at a small table outside a blue cottage. They were locked in conversation and almost unaware of our presence. I silently followed Rhey. I wondered what new adventure awaited us in this village. Surely, it would be something calmer, quieter.

"Oh good, you're here," Saraiyah's voice called kindly as we approached the table. "This is Alli, the sojourner I was telling you about," she said to the maiden.

The maiden smiled and extended her hand, welcoming me. "My name is Rose. Won't you please join us?"

Rhey nodded and smiled, "I must tend to our steed. If you will excuse me," he said with a brief bow and a glance at Rose. He turned and walked toward the back, Swift following closely behind.

Saraiyah's colors shone and sparkled, revealing her excitement. "Alli, we were just discussing giving you your next treasure," she said with enthusiasm. "This is for your journey." She tenderly pulled out a small leather-bound book and gave it to me. She smiled, "This is the King's Chronicles, the book of all books. It is the story of the Great King and His kingdom."

This book must be very important; I felt the respect in her voice.

"There are many stories about our world in this book, including the story of the steward and the snake. Remember," she said rather mysteriously, "this book is not from your world." Then she opened the cover, tore out the first page, and handed it to me. "Eat it," she said.

How was I supposed to read a book that I ate? What in the world? Saraiyah stood over me, tapping her foot, waiting for me to obey. Okay. She wanted me to eat it. Fine. I would eat it. I rolled the page into a little ball and popped it into my mouth. I expected the taste of hundred-year-old paper to offend my taste buds, but instead, something crazy happened: the page dissolved on my tongue, and images flashed across my mind. Many scenes unfolded before me: a father bent over a cradle, kissing a baby's cheek; Saraiyah hand-in-hand gently guiding a lost, crying little girl; a world forming with earthquakes, stars, moons, oceans, and a sun.

All the scenes unfolded quickly like those nature shows using time-lapse photography, revealing a flower blooming within seconds. I was fascinated.

The scenes paused momentarily, and when they resumed, a faraway land with a teenage boy and a giant filled my view. The giant looked very angry, and the teen seemed very small. I noticed the youth had a slingshot in his pocket. He pulled the slingshot from his pocket and readied it with a rock. He spun it around and let the rock fly, hitting the giant right between the eyes! Falling, the defeated giant slammed hard, shaking the ground. The youth's victory yell echoed as he ran toward the giant while the scene darkened. I heard ominous music like the beginning of a scary movie. My heart pounded as the curtain lifted; *what was coming next?* Then I saw him...the snake I had encountered. He walked on two legs and spoke with a man and a woman. It sent chills down my spine. Multiple scenes whizzed past quickly. Abruptly, it was over. Whew!

"All done?" Saraiyah asked. "Good! That was the table of contents!"

"Say *what* now?" I asked, astonished. I sat back. Just the table of contents?

"Alli, this book is more than mere stories. You will find everything you need for your journey within its pages. It has *the* way of life in it. If you let it perform its good work in you, it will even lead you home. All you have to do," she continued, "is eat it!"

Not a bad deal. Just eat the book. Compared to other things I ate in their world, the page was kind of bland, but

I could deal with that. The stories seemed so cool, better than any movie or TV show I'd ever seen. I tucked the book into my trusty backpack and waited.

"Okay, dear one. I want you to stay here and rest for a little while. Take some time to write about your adventures in your journal. I think it will be helpful for you down the road. Use the time to think about everything that has happened so far. Don't forget to read your new book. I must attend to a matter for the King. I will see you soon." And with that, she was gone, disappeared right before our eyes. I blinked dumbly, still unused to how things happened here.

"Well then, let's get you some food," Rose suggested.

Food! Now she was talking! Since I had just eaten a piece of paper, food sounded pretty good! I liked Rose already and followed her inside. The cottage was simple but lovely. A fire was burning in the large stone fireplace, making the room warm and cozy. I could tell it was used for warmth and cooking. I spied a delicious cake cooling on a cupboard. Rose saw me eyeing the cake and smiled. She stepped over to the cupboard, cut two generous slices of cake, and poured two glasses of milk. She invited me to sit with her at a small table near the window. A single rose in a bud vase sat in the middle of the table. She waited till I was seated and sat down. Rose smiled at me while taking a bite of the cake. As cake crumbs dropped from her fork to the table, she giggled.

Without embarrassment, she said, "Pardon me, Mistress."

I saw the humor in her pretty green eyes and breathed a sigh of relief. I realized I didn't have to be perfect for Rose and relaxed. I wondered if she did that on purpose to set me at ease.

After she politely dabbed her mouth with her napkin, she said, "Miss Alli, please tell me about yourself."

I replied, hesitating, "There isn't much to tell since I'm only thirteen."

"What is life like where you're from? Tell me about it," she prompted.

Talking with Rose felt natural and easy. Unlike back at home, I didn't stammer or stutter when I spoke with her. Maybe it was her beauty or her friendly personality, or maybe it was being in a different world; whatever it was, it was nice. I thoroughly enjoyed my talk with Rose. Was this what it felt like to have a friend?

TROUBLE IN PARADISE

Funny how things changed. Later that day in the village, I was bored. I usually craved a simple, uncomplicated, day-to-day routine. But now, after all the adventures and coming and going, I was bored with no action. I decided to explore my surroundings.

Meandering outside Rose's home, I found a small stable, where Swift was resting. Greeting him with a carrot, I pet his muzzle. Swift's nod and snort made me think he was glad I was there. I think we were becoming friends. On the other side of the stable were more horses in the meadow. The barn had the usual geese, chickens, milk cows, and a barn cat with kittens. It had average run-of-the-mill farm animals: no fairies with wings or talking lambs. After getting my fill of petting them, I headed off for more exploring.

Not far from the barn was a partially overgrown path. I was curious to see what was ahead of me. Maybe the path would reveal some hints? Tiptoeing onto it, making sure to avoid the ivy, I only intended to walk a few steps just to see what was out there. Guiltily, I remembered Saraiyah asked me to read the book and write in my journal. Ugh, I hated journaling. *You can get it done later*, I reassured myself.

The path's entrance had a thick forest whose tall leafy trees filtered out most of the sunlight. The cobblestone lane was wide enough for several carts to travel back and forth. This had to be the main road to and from the village. I convinced myself it was likely the route for my next travels. So, I let myself explore further. Saraiyah's warning flashed through my head, "Always stay on the path, don't go off by yourself!" I let her words rattle around for a moment but dismissed them. I hadn't gone very far, and I'd only go a little further, I justified. What could be the harm in that? Maybe it was my stubborn streak or my used to being alone that made me ignore Saraiyah's warning. But I continued.

A small child was bouncing a ball a few steps down the path. Suddenly it rolled off the trail into the leaves carpeting the forest floor. How odd? How did he get out here by himself? I figured I better recover his ball and get him back to where he belonged, wherever *that* was. He shouldn't be out here alone, I concluded.

"Would you like some help?" I offered and stepped onto the leaves to help him fetch his ball. He was seven or eight years old, not much more.

Within moments of stepping onto the leaves, I began to sink. Down I went, further and further. The leaves were not just a few inches deep, and before I knew it, I had sunk up to my neck. What was going on? I was perplexed and frightened. I felt like I was drowning. "Help!" I cried.

I looked at the little boy; he glared back at me with a red gleam in his eyes. Shivers went down my spine. "Oh, too sad. I am sorry. I can't help you, Mistress," he sneered and ran off into the forest.

Saraiyah's words of warning flooded back to me. She said the enemy would come disguised so I wouldn't recognize him. *That* was *not* a little boy, and *this* was *not* the main road in town! And I was in trouble! As I tried to figure a way out of the situation, the trees came to life; their roots and ivy tendrils wrapped around me. They dragged me deeper and deeper into the pit of leaves.

"*Help me!*" I cried again, "*Help!*" I didn't have my trumpet or my backpack. The lamb gave me the trumpet to sound if I ever got in trouble. How could I be so stupid! How foolish I'd been! First, I went off alone without Rhey, and then I left my backpack at the house.

"I'm so sorry! Ima! Rhey! Please, please help me. I'm so stupid," I cried, "I know I've been foolish. I shouldn't have left without your permission or gone off alone! Help me, please!" Tears stained my face as I pleaded for help.

Then, out of the darkness, I heard the dreaded voice: the snake. "I hear you, and *I am* here for you. I am all the help you need," he hissed. His stench and fear filled me as his hateful voice penetrated my thoughts. I heard him slithering and hissing, but I couldn't see him.

"You are lossst, poor thing. Come, little one, sssee, I'll be better to you than anyone from the King. If He is ssso good and kind, why hasssn't He come to meet you Himself? He hasss only sssent Hisss lowly servantsss to you. Obviousssly, He doesn't think very much of you, doesss He?" he hissed.

His voice became more convincing as the ivy wrapped tighter and the leaves covered me. He made a good point. Why hadn't the Great King greeted me Himself? If I was so special, He would have. I left my home and everything familiar to travel here. Maybe, I *was* better off dead. I shouldn't have come here!

Like wispy tendrils of ivy, the poisonous thoughts filled my head, hiding the truths from Saraiyah. The toxic mist, like smoke, had filled my lungs and penetrated my thoughts. I shouldn't have come to this place. Then in a moment, bright as the dawn, I remembered my mom told me I would be safe in this world. But *this* was *not* safe!

Stunned and terrified, I considered everything. What if it was all a lie? I believed I was safe with Saraiyah and Rhey. I believed Rose was my friend. If they really loved me, they wouldn't have left me here alone. My thoughts turned into accusations. Why did they allow me to be tempted to come here? Didn't they know I would be curious? Didn't they know I would want to explore things?

At the welcome feast, the lamb told me I was wanted and welcomed in their world. The snake slithered closer to me, interrupting my thoughts. His horrible smell filled my nostrils and rested heavily upon me. The dread I felt was replaced by numbness. I didn't know if the snake had poisoned me as snakes are known to do or if the vines were too tight, but I couldn't breathe. I just couldn't breathe.

All at once, I heard a trumpet blast and horse hooves

galloping down the path.

"Back away, vermin! Be gone with you, I say!"

Oh yay! I recognized Rhey's voice. He had come for me!

"You know this one is under the protection of the Great King!" he confidently declared.

"Well, if she'sss under the protection of the King," the snake hissed loudly, "ssshe gave up that right when she left the path. Ssshe came here to me."

"Hush!" Rhey commanded. "You know the King has paid the blood price. I'm here to redeem her in His name. Be gone now, in the Great King's name!" he declared.

I heard Swift snorting and stomping his hooves. He trampled the leaves near the snake, making him hiss and slither away.

Rhey alighted Swift. "Are you all right, Mistress?" he asked tenderly.

"I…I…I am okay now," I stuttered shakily.

Rhey carefully cut off the vines and tree roots that imprisoned me. I cried and trembled as the numbness wore off.

"Whatever possessed you to come here in the first place?" Rhey sighed.

"I was curious and bored," I said with a sniff.

"Well," he said, "come, Mistress." He pulled me out

of what surely would have been an early grave. I shook the disgusting leaves from my clothing as he hoisted me onto Swift's back. I marveled at Swift's magnificence as he stood there quiet and still. What would have happened if I hadn't been rescued? I shuddered at the thought.

Rhey jumped onto Swift's back. "Hold on tight!" he commanded. He did not have to tell me twice; I did not want to fall off. I had enough excitement for one day. I wasn't bored now! I just wanted to leave this horrible place and return to the safety and warmth of Rose's cottage.

I held tightly to Rhey as we sped through the forest. I closed my eyes to protect them from the wind beating against my face. I sensed a bright light beaming through my eyelids, like when you turn your face toward the sun. I opened my eyes and saw a flashing light. I couldn't tell what it was, but it was coming right at us! The whole sky lit up like high noon, causing me to squint from the brightness. I narrowed my eyes and realized it was Saraiyah flying toward us with her wings ablaze. Awestruck by her brilliance and beauty, I felt a lump rise in my throat. Oh no! I was disobedient. I did the exact opposite of what she told me to do. What would she think? Would she be disappointed, angry, or even worse, sad? Would she still like me? The lump in my throat got so big I could barely swallow. I had really messed up.

Swift slowed to a methodic trot and then stood still on the path. Saraiyah swooped in and fluttered down beside us, her wings and body aglow with color. "There, there now, child," she spoke softly, "it will all be okay."

She reached out and tenderly touched my hand as she spoke. Immediately, the baseball-sized lump in my throat melted. All the fear faded with her gentle touch, and unconditional love and calm covered me like dew on my skin. My eyes glistened with tears from her response. She wasn't mad even when I didn't listen to her? Saraiyah gently lifted my chin and looked into my eyes. I had never known such kindness, except my mom's. I was relieved she wasn't mad at me, but it wasn't easy. When I got in trouble, it was usually at school. I'd get yelled at, made to feel ashamed, and that was the end of it. Disappointed and angry red-faced adults were the norm when I blew it. Her reaction was so different, making me never want to disobey her again.

"Even though this is an important lesson, we don't need to talk about it right now. Let's get you home," Saraiyah said.

Back at the cottage, Rose served us a homey meal. After dinner, I sat by the hearth and watched the fire, mesmerized by the dancing flames and crackling wood. I was deep in thought when Saraiyah joined me. "What have you learned today?" she asked.

I frowned and paused for a moment, "I have learned not to go off without my backpack, for starters."

Saraiyah chuckled, "That's good. Anything else?"

"Yes," I sighed, "I learned not to go anywhere without your permission. I won't go anyplace until you've said it's okay." I dared to sneak a peek at Saraiyah. Her face was even more stunning in the glow of the flames. She gently reached over and took my hand. I timidly looked at her; I was still nervous about disappointing her.

In my fleeting glance, our eyes met.

"Alli, you truly have the most beautiful eyes, especially in this light."

I couldn't believe it! Here I was, waiting for a lecture, but instead, I got a compliment?

"Thank you," I mumbled shyly. My anxiety lessened with the kindness of her gaze.

"The time will come when you will have more freedom. You must understand: you have a very great destiny. As you walk this path, you will learn many things that will equip and empower you. You will learn your purpose and discover your true identity. Please know we don't require you to grovel; your world would say, 'lick our boots' when you make mistakes. Our kingdom doesn't work that way. It's important to say sorry and make amends, but knowing you're loved and belong comes first. Our guidance is simply to keep you safe and help you gain all the experiences you need for your life's journey."

"I know," I said remorsefully. "I am so sorry." Tears snuck from the corners of my eyes before I could stop them.

"It is okay, dear one," Saraiyah comforted me. "Sometimes, the hardest lessons are your best lessons. You don't forget them quite so easily. What you think and feel is important. We want you to think for yourself, but remember, every decision has an outcome, a consequence. As you make decisions, you learn what happens with each choice and grow. Do you remember when I told you, 'Every day you are alive is a gift'?"

"Yes, I remember."

"Today was a good example of this. Dry your eyes and remember, we love you. Now, off to bed with you, okay?"

"Okay," I sniffed and wiped my tears on my sleeve.

TOGETHERNESS?

In the morning, at the end of breakfast, Rhey leaned over and kissed Rose, thanking her for the meal. What just happened? Boy, was I surprised! Saraiyah must have seen the shock on my face because she quickly explained.

"It is fine, Alli. They are married," she chuckled.

"Wow! I had no idea," I muttered to Rose. Rhey was apparently more tight-lipped than me about personal stuff. We had spent a bunch of time together, but he never said a thing. I didn't know he was married to anyone, let alone Rose.

Rose looked at me and giggled, "I should have told you yesterday, but it slipped my mind in all the excitement over your, umm, shall we say, 'adventure.' We've been married a little over a year. I keep the home fires burning for my knight," she lovingly glanced toward Rhey, "while he escorts sojourners, like yourself, to the castle." Rhey seemed embarrassed as he grinned at me. Rose continued, "Our village, The Keepers' Way, begins a more difficult portion of the journey. The Great King knew this was a good stopping point for travelers to rest and refresh."

I sat and absorbed all the new information. There was never a dull moment in this world; it was full of surprises.

"Umm, pardon me," I hesitated, "You said, 'travelers.' Are others joining us here?"

"Why yes, Mistress," Rhey smiled, "some travelers are joining us before we continue our journey."

Oh no! my mind screamed. I just got used to traveling with Rhey, Saraiyah, and Swift. I was starting to know what to expect: Rhey led quietly and confidently, Saraiyah reminded me of my mom and put me at ease, and Swift, well, was just amazing. Who wouldn't want to play and horse around with Swift? We were a team. I had become comfortable traveling with them, but traveling with a whole group of strangers—that was *not* for me! I couldn't do that!

I took a deep breath and exhaled slowly. Maybe if I just sat back, laid low, and faded into the background, I would be okay. I decided to trust my usual routine to get me through, just like at home. Invisibility.

Instantly, I was hungry, and it was time to turn to my real source of comfort, food! I dismissed my concerns and asked Rose if she had more cookies left. Rose did not disappoint; she had some left from dessert last night. After eating, what could only be described as a "bunch" of cookies, I went out to sit on the cottage porch. My belly was bursting, so I laid back against the chair and sleepily gazed into the garden. Rose's delicious cookies certainly hit the spot and, for the moment, calmed my nerves.

"Alli," Saraiyah whispered.

"Hmmm?" I replied sleepily from my cookie daze.

"Would it be all right if I sat and talked with you?"

"Sure," I sat up in my chair and shook the sleepiness from my head.

"Alli, how do you feel about more travelers joining us?"

"Okay," I lied.

"Alli, is that true?"

She moved closer and looked me directly in the eyes. Vibrant purples, blues, and swirls of white light flashed in her eyes, startling me as I looked back at her. Her eyes were pulling me in…toward life. Then I remembered the serpent loves lies. I didn't want anything to do with that. I could not lie to her again.

Catching my breath, I admitted, "Well, no. Na…na…not really," I stuttered.

"Just as I thought," she said knowingly. "Alli, why do you think you are so uncomfortable being around people?"

"I don't know. I just am," I sighed, "always have been."

"May I tell you a secret?" Saraiyah asked.

"Sure," I shrugged, trying to be cool, but she had my attention now.

"You weren't designed that way."

"Huh? What do you mean?" Designed? I wasn't

designed. I was just born.

"Oh, I just know a few things about the way you were made. You are not meant to be alone or isolated. Have you noticed how everything in life is connected? It is extremely rare for life to be sustained without connecting in some way with other living things."

As she finished speaking, a vast array of pictures flooded my mind. There were images of lawyers, teachers, school kids, police officers, and firefighters. Children were playing together, kittens running after each other, businesspeople conversing with one another, and bees hovering over flowers. A beautiful lioness was lying with her cub, his front leg and paw over her shoulder. Next was a stream beside a row of trees. The tree's roots reached the water's edge, sipping the rushing water. Last were a mother and a father gazing at their baby with so much love in their eyes. They were a family, which made my heart ache. I couldn't help but wish my dad was still around. Did my parents adore me when I was little?

"Alli," Saraiyah continued, "you are created to connect with other people. Relationship is what life is all about. The dark one works hard to destroy friendships, tear families apart, and disconnect communities of all living things. He knows the power of community, and he works against it night and day. I know you are unhappy about more travelers joining us, but I ask you to be open and willing to meet new people. Getting to know new people can help you get to know yourself better. You might learn a few things. Will you trust me, Alli?"

How could I say no to Saraiyah?

"You are created for more, and you can have more if you are willing to pay the price, darling girl."

Pay the price? I didn't like the sound of that!

"But I didn't bring any money!" I objected.

Saraiyah laughed, "No, my dear, not that kind of price. Sometimes a price is something you give in exchange for something better. In this case, your comfort zone is the price. Are you willing to be uncomfortable around new people for the sake of relationships? Will you set aside your own comfort to gain something precious like a community? If you are willing to do these things, you will open yourself to wonderful possibilities. You may even realize your heart's desire, a true best friend." Saraiyah leaned over and hugged me. Peace washed over me, and I melted into her arms. She let go and looked at me with a huge smile. "It will all work out. Just wait and see."

TOO MANY PEOPLE

In the morning came the alarming sound of people in the yard outside Rose's cottage. Stunned, I stared out the window. People were everywhere, noisy and chaotic. I shrunk back, ran to my bed, and hid under the covers. The familiar icy tentacles of fear wrapped around my heart. *What am I going to do?* my mind cried. My heart raced as my breath came in gasps. Taking a deep breath in and out, I slowed my breathing. As the din lessened, I decided to look back out the window. Maybe if I focused on just a few travelers, one at a time, it wouldn't be so bad. I considered Saraiyah's words. Was I willing to pay the price for something wonderful? I wanted to answer yes, so I gritted my teeth and determined to try.

Okay, who should I focus on? I spotted a family of three, dressed in peasant clothes, standing alone in the distance. The father was scowling, the baby was crying, and the mom looked stressed out. Honestly, they seemed as miserable as me. Mental note: steer clear of them!

As I scanned the crowd, a commotion in the middle of

the yard grabbed my attention. A girl about my age was yelling and waving her hands around. She was throwing an absolute hissy fit, smack-dab in the middle of everyone. Wow! Who was she? Didn't she have any pride? She had dark black hair and a turned-up nose. Maybe some people would think she was pretty, but her look of disgust twisted her face into an ugly mask. I definitely didn't like her. Mental note number two: steer clear of her too!

A very tall man stood out in the crowd. Like literally, he towered about eight inches above everyone else. His clothing looked royal with simple elegance. His long, blond hair was pulled back with a leather strap at the base of his neck, revealing his kind, handsome face dignified with a nicely trimmed goatee. He looked confident but not full of himself like a lot of guys. My guess was he was in charge.

"What do you think of him?" Saraiyah asked as she quietly slid beside me.

"Who?" I puzzled.

"The man you were just watching?" I learned not to question how Saraiyah knew things. She knew stuff, and I was learning just to accept it.

"I don't know. I haven't met him or anything," I replied.

"Alli, I only asked what you *think* of him."

"Oh," I wasn't used to sharing my thoughts with anyone. I shrugged, "Umm, he looks nice."

Saraiyah's laughter tinkled on the air and sprinkled me like misty raindrops. The familiar grip of fear loosened its hold on me. I could breathe more easily. Her laughter felt so wonderful that I wanted her to laugh again! And she did.

"Feel better now?" she chuckled, turning her gaze to me.

"Uh-huh," I said. A little giggle and then a full laugh escaped my lips. I couldn't hold it back. How did Saraiyah always make me feel so much better?

"Good! Are you ready?" She took my hand, led me out the door, and walked right into the center of all the commotion.

"Oh my!" I exclaimed. I couldn't resist her pull, but I was not happy about it. It felt like being thrown into the deep end of the pool. Sink or swim! I didn't want to sink. Saraiyah took me places I wouldn't go otherwise. Before I realized where we were heading, we were already there. In front of me stood the obnoxious girl from earlier.

"Miss Alli, this is Miss Raven. Miss Raven, this is Miss Alli."

I stood there for a few moments. Raven's look of disgust didn't deter me from staring at her remarkable sapphire blue eyes. They held my attention, even though everything inside me wanted to look away.

"Hi," Raven tartly said as she scowled with contempt. Oh, I really did not like her. I shrank behind the walls around my heart. Much to my relief, Saraiyah led me away from Raven and over to the tall man.

"Miss Alli, I am truly pleased to introduce you to Prince Trueheart. Prince Trueheart, this is Maiden Alli." She leaned in close and whispered, "He's a prince of the realm. He will be joining our group."

"Ni…nice to meet you," I stammered, staring at his vest, my eyes refusing to look up any further. I just could not look at his face.

"It is a pleasure to meet you, Miss Alli," he said with a flourish and a bow as he gently grasped my hand. For the first time in my life, I realized I was meeting a very great man. As he rose from his bow, he peered into my eyes. Wonder beyond wonders, it seemed as though he was in awe of me…awe…of me?

"You have very lovely eyes, Milady. They are quite unusual to see." His pleasant smile relaxed me, but I still didn't know what to say. Thankfully, Saraiyah asked him a question, which diverted his attention. I retreated behind her and waited quietly.

As she led me back to the house, she asked, "How do you feel about all these people?"

"I don't know if I can do this," I confessed.

"Will it help to know they are not all going with you?" Saraiyah comforted.

"Well, yeah, it would."

"Remember, Alli: all your needs will be met. I invite you to trust our Great King's heart. He knows your needs better than you do. We have handpicked who will travel together. You see, Alli, some of the travelers need you as much as you need them. When facing the challenges ahead, remember you are here for a reason. Your presence makes a difference," Saraiyah assured me, "It will be all right. You will see."

And with that, she left me to find quiet in Rose's home.

POOR, POOR ALLI

I went to my room in the back of the cottage to disappear.
I couldn't handle it anymore. There were just too many
people. I buried my face in the pillow, muffling my sobs,
and cried. What was I going to do? I wanted to change, but
this was too hard. As the pressure built, I just wanted to go
home.

My thoughts raced, and I started feeling sorry for myself.
Did I ask for any of this? No. I did not. At that moment, I
heard the dreaded snaky voice, "Sssee, I told you it would
be thisss way. They don't care about you! Poor, poor Alli.
Why don't you leave this place? You don't have to put up
with thisss!"

*He's right. It isn't fair! No one ever told me I'd be
surrounded by strangers and have to travel with them. No
one told me it would be this hard. Can I find my own way
back to my house? Maybe I should do just that.*

The snaky voice seeped more deeply into my mind,
"Yesss, run back home. I will help you. You'll sssee."
A dark mist filled the room. As I breathed it in, a heavy

blanket of sadness covered me. I buried my face deeper into my pillow. I didn't want anyone to hear me, but I was sobbing and sobbing. I couldn't stop.

A light knock at the door interrupted my pity party. "Alli?" Rose spoke softly, "Alli, are you okay?"

"Just a minute," my voice quivered. Giving my eyes a quick wipe on my sleeve, I sniffled and searched for something to blow my nose. A tissue container sat on the bedside table, yelling that 'The King supplies all my needs.' Angrily, I grabbed a tissue and quietly blew my nose. I had to get it together.

"Alli? Alli?" Rose gently persisted. When she called my name this time, the dark mist lifted, and my mind began to clear. I remembered Rhey and Saraiyah told me they'd be with me. So, what did I have to worry about? Wasn't this better than all the times of being sad and lonely at home?

"Pardon me, Miss Alli, may I come in?" Rose gently inquired.

I managed an okay.

Rose peered around the door, "Miss Alli, would you be so kind as to join me in the kitchen to help prepare some bread?"

"Umm. Yes. Just a minute, please."

With a smile and a nod of her pretty head, Rose said, "You can join me when you are ready, Mistress."

I steadied myself and tried to get it together. I climbed

out of bed and headed to the washbasin on the table. Admiring the blue and white flowers on the sides of the basin, I splashed my face with water. The coolness was a welcome blast to my tear-stained face. I quickly ran my fingers through my unruly hair. Boy, was I a mess! *Okay, Alli, get it together!* I took a big, deep breath, left my tear fest behind, and joined Rose in the kitchen.

During the next few hours of baking, I discovered the joy of helping others. Rose made baking and serving so much fun it didn't even feel like work. She laughed and joked. She was so happy about baking bread for other people it rubbed off on me. Pretty soon, we were both laughing and giggling. Who knew kneading dough (which I discovered was hard work) would teach me such great things?

"Rose, are we making all the food for the travelers?"

"Why, no!" she replied, "That isn't possible. Each person brings what they have. Everyone contributes something. Some will give more, some will give less, but it always ends up being enough."

"Tha...tha...that's super cool," I managed to stammer.

"But why didn't I have to bring anything on my journey here?"

Rose paused before she answered, "Well, perhaps it's because you were coming such a great distance. Or you didn't have anything to bring. Sometimes," she hesitated, "sometimes the King doesn't have you bring anything. So, you will learn how to rely upon Him. One thing I know for sure. Our King knows everything each one needs to complete their journey. So that's what He does!"

As I looked at her, a smile on her face, flour on her nose, and a loose strand of hair, I wondered if there was ever a lovelier woman than Rose.

"My, it's getting late. You may want to go to bed. Tomorrow is a big day. You will be taking your leave to continue your journey." Rose exclaimed.

I thanked Rose and sleepily went off to bed. Today had been hard with all the people, but it sure ended well in Rose's kitchen. I couldn't help drifting off to sleep with a smile on my face.

THE LION'S ROAR

At the break of dawn, the loud noises of activity and the horses stamping and snorting in the yard interrupted my sleep. Yawning, I made my way to the window. Men and women were busy loading their goods on the pack mules, preparing for the journey. The low murmurs of their voices sounded like a hum through my window. The kids ran around playfully as the adults rushed about. The horses were saddled and ready to go. What a busy morning! Before panic set in, Saraiyah was by my side. I slowly exhaled, relieved and comforted by her presence. She amazed me.

"Good morning, Alli," she leaned in to kiss my cheek.

"Why, uh, good morning!" I managed, startled by the kiss.

"How did you sleep?"

"I slept well," I just didn't mention the horrible part *before* sleep.

"How was your time after I left you yesterday?" she asked pointedly.

"Umm, uh," I hesitated, recalling my promise not to lie to Saraiyah again. "Not...not so good," I replied slowly.

Saraiyah looked at me tenderly, "Yesterday was another battle you fought well."

"Battle? I fought well? I don't understand."

"I know, my darling girl, but you will understand soon enough. It is time to go. Are you ready?"

A quiet "wow" escaped my lips when we made our way outside. The yard was busy but much emptier than yesterday. So many people were already gone. An odd, painful tug pulled on my heart. Why wasn't I relieved there were fewer people? What had gotten into me? There were still a few familiar faces: Raven and the kindly man. What was his name? Oh yeah, Prince Trueheart...also the couple with the baby. Despite all the activity, they seemed calmer today. There were a few new faces: three little boys ran around, their mother chasing after them; a man, maybe their father, was chatting with Rhey; and lastly, a lovely lady with her belongings and toddler in a small wagon. I didn't know the total, but the group was a fraction of the crowd from yesterday.

Despite the hustle and bustle of preparations, nothing was out of place. There was an odd neatness and orderliness about it all. The yard showed no evidence of the large gathering from the last two days—no trash lying on the ground. There wasn't even any horse mess left behind. It was weird; I'd seen the effects of large crowds before: a local fair, a music festival, a party, a movie...afterward *all* messes, but here...nothing was out of place.

"May I have everyone's attention, please?" Rhey's call interrupted me. I was glad to see him; he hadn't been around the past few days. Had he been gathering more travelers?

We responded to his call for order and drew closer. "All gather 'round. I have an announcement to make." A hush fell across the yard, except for the mother, struggling to get her three young boys to stand still. Rhey continued, "The King is very grateful you have chosen to join us on our journey to the Banquet of the Great King. He graciously extends His favor to you. We still have a distance to go before our journey's end. The King determined it would be best for us to travel together through the Dark Wilderness."

Dark Wilderness? I didn't like the sound of that.

After Rhey finished speaking, I tucked myself tightly against Swift, hiding from the crowd, pondering what the Dark Wilderness could be. The next thing I knew, Raven found me in my little hiding place. She boldly walked over to me and whispered loudly, "That's terrible. I hope we don't get lost there. They say, 'Once you go into the Dark Wilderness, you never return.' I am not sure if going there is such a good idea." She stared at me, waiting for my reply.

Glancing at Raven, I didn't say a word, as usual. I stepped back from her, hoping she'd leave me alone if I ignored her. Meanwhile, Rhey was still speaking.

"It is with great honor that I introduce you to the King's dear friend, Sir Reynald."

Sir Reynald? What a surprise! Sir Reynald was the lamb from the welcome feast, who gave me the beautiful trumpet. He wore a cornflower blue silk coat with black buttons and a white collar. His pants perfectly matched his jacket; he looked so regal. Was he a prince of the realm too? He was so humble; it was hard to tell. The gold aura, though, should have been a clue there was more to him than met the eye.

Sir Reynald nodded to Prince Trueheart, signaling him to proceed. Prince Trueheart stepped forward and cleared his throat. In a rich tone, he proclaimed, "Milords and Miladies, it is time for you to meet the King's one true son, Prince Boqer Aster. It is my privilege and honor to make Him known to you all. You may address Him as Prince Boqer."

On that queue, a band of knights stepped out of the forest into our midst. They reminded me of our high-school marching band. They stood in perfectly aligned rows: the first row of knights held flags, the second had trumpets, and the third held drums. They marched in unison until they stood in front of Sir Reynald and Prince Trueheart. After a few moments, the last row drummed a beat, and the band of knights parted again in unison. In the center of the twelve knights stood the most awesome...lion. A lion?

"Huh?" I puzzled quietly. Was the Great King a beast? Then I remembered Saraiyah's wise words: "Not all is as it seems."

An explosion of voices rang out, filling the air, "Yay! He's here; our Prince is here!"

As excited murmurs ran through the crowd, Rose delicately stepped through everyone. Seemingly sure of herself, she boldly walked up to the lion. Bringing a basket of our baked bread with her, Rose curtsied before Him. Prince Boqer was smiling as He held out His paw and handed her a beautiful bouquet of red roses. That was so cool! Roses for Rose.

Well, there was a lion, a lamb, and now all that was missing was the...Oh my! There he was, walking up to the lion and the lamb...the child! Right there in front of me stood the three "people" from my dream. Who knew I would see them again? Weird! Would I ever get over the weirdness in this place? Were the lion and lamb in front of me the same ones from my trumpet? From the park benches? From the many places where I'd seen their images? *They must be celebrities*, I thought. *How exciting!*

Saraiyah glided over to me, "Come, Alli, let me introduce you."

"Oh...Oh, okay," I dumbly mumbled as I followed behind Saraiyah. I wanted to tell her I was afraid of the lion, but she moved so quickly I couldn't get the words out.

"My Lord," Saraiyah stated, "here is my charge, Alli." She bowed low to the ground and backed away.

I stood alone in front of the massive beast, trembling; my knees were knocking together. My heart pounded in my chest as my eyes glued to my feet. I was too scared to look up.

Gently, He spoke to me, "There, there, little one, I won't bite. I don't even like meat, least of all, human." He chuckled lightly, and my fear eased. A blanket of calm wrapped around me from head to feet. I wobbled a bit, almost falling over. But why? Was it because of the lion? He laughed again, causing the ground to shake. Then He said, "Alli, you are a true delight. Will you scratch My head?"

So startled by His request, I forgot to keep my eyes on my feet. Looking up, I stared right into His majestic face. Mirth twinkled in His fiery eyes; a light breeze teased and ruffled His mane. He stood there, looking bold and beautiful, a magnificent gold crown adorning His head. I was overwhelmed by His beauty...by the sheer fact that He was, after all, a *lion*!

Holding my breath, I tensed every muscle in my body, then carefully stretched out my hand and lightly tapped the lion's head.

"One more time, little one. There's more in you than that!"

Oh, brother! There wasn't more in me than that! I took a deep breath before I exhaled. The lion roared suddenly, causing the ground to shake all around us. The vibrations traveled from the ground into my body like electricity, all the way to my head. I boldly shot out my hand and scratched His ear.

"Oh! Ho, ho, Alli, that is perfect!"

I stood there amazed, not believing what had just happened. I wanted to return to my regular routine and stare at my feet, but I couldn't stop looking at this fascinating beast. The effects of His roar must have lingered because

I boldly asked, "Are You the King's son? The one I am supposed to meet?"

"Why yes, Alli, I am the King's one true son," He said, smiling at me. "I am heir to everything you see. My great Father is the King of kings. Everyone who accepts Our invitation is a part of Our wonderful family."

What did He mean by *that*? Did that include me? I could not stop looking at His beautiful face.

Sir Reynald, the lamb, came over and said, "Good to see you again, Miss Alli. We are so very proud of you."

"Oh! Thank you!" I blurted out, stunned by my quick reply.

The child from earlier walked up to the lion. Studying him a bit closer, I realized I had seen him before: first in my dream and then at the welcome feast. I grinned at the memory of us laughing and laughing together after the feast. He started to climb atop the lion, giggling and jumping. The lion lowered himself to help the boy climb aboard. Then they playfully rolled around together, laughing happily, and ignoring the rest of us. It seemed like they were freshly reunited, long-lost friends.

After a few moments of horseplay, the lion stood up on all fours and said, "Okay, time to go, My children. Gather round." Everyone scrambled to their feet and stood in a circle around the mighty lion. Prince Boqer walked around the circle and roared over each and every one of us, one by one.

A RIDE IN THE SKIES

"Milady, our King has ordered for you to ride with me. Here you go," Rhey said as he pulled me onto Swift.

"But what about the others?" I sputtered.

I couldn't believe what had just come out of my mouth! Since when did I care about the others? Usually, I was more worried about making myself invisible than caring about others. I looked around to make sure everyone had a mode of travel. The family with the baby was in a horse-drawn wagon. Raven sat proudly on top of a beautiful chestnut mare. Prince Trueheart, unbelievably, sat astride a unicorn. A unicorn? What was next? Spaceships? I laughed to myself. Nah, that would be silly.

The lion roared again, shaking the ground and vibrating through me. What an awesome sound! I could not get over it. Strength flowed through me with every roar, making me stronger than ever before.

"Are you ready, Mistress?" Rhey asked. Before I could even nod a quick yes, he continued, "Hold on!" And with that, we were off.

At the beginning of the path, Swift trotted confidently, but then wonders beyond wonders—wings appeared out of Swift's sides. Before I could figure out what was happening, Swift began galloping at a breakneck pace. Moments later, Swift flapped his magnificent wings, and we lifted off the ground. Oh my! Oh my! Oh my! I couldn't believe my eyes. How was it possible? Where was he hiding those wings?

Once in the air, I looked around. Why were we the only ones flying while everyone else was walking or riding? I gulped the air as we flew higher and higher toward the sun. Rhey circled above the group, each loop growing wider and wider. His eyes narrowed as he focused intently on the ground below. Was he figuring out which path to take? No, he was looking for something with his intent stare. It hit me! The enemy! He was looking far and wide for the enemy!

"Hold on, Alli," he yelled back to me as Swift dove toward the ground. Whoa! This was much better than any kiddie ride at the fair. I tightened my grip on Rhey's waist and held on for dear life. We were going so fast. How on earth were we going to land? *Please don't crash*, I prayed. Abruptly, Swift slowed way down and hovered, like a helicopter, over the ground. Gracefully, gently, he glided down. We landed safely with a bump and a little step. I let out a big sigh of relief. Whew!

Swift trotted directly over to Prince Trueheart. Rhey gave his report of all he saw. I focused on his voice, trying to calm my racing and pounding heart. "All is clear for the next thirty miles. The Dark Forest shows no enemy activity." Well, that was good to hear. The men continued talking for a few minutes before Rhey turned his attention back to me, "If you're okay, Mistress, we will continue."

"Umm, sure," I replied, subdued by the ride.

Rhey and I rode Swift to the back of the group, behind the women and children, while Prince Trueheart and a few men led the group from the front. After my exciting flight, I was a little disappointed plodding along behind the women and children. Being in the back was like having the air let out of my balloon. I didn't mind not being in the lead, though. That was where the enemy would attack first (or so I thought). Prince Trueheart was the perfect person to protect us. He was brave and strong. Valiant! Yes, that was the perfect word to describe him. Valiant! I would have to look it up when I got back to school, but I was pretty sure that was the right word. It felt weird to think about home. Since being caught up in this world, I hadn't thought about home much. What would life be like when I got back home?

Would I be happy at home, after all this? My mom had been on this journey, and she was happy. Maybe I would be happy too, like my mom. I was glad she had her journey first. No, "happy" wasn't the right word..."content," yes, "content" was a better word to describe her. Mom didn't get upset about anything; she just smiled and kept going. Maybe when all this was over, I would be content. At that moment, I felt hope flicker in my heart. *Was I changing from my old, sad self into something happy and new?* Hmmm. The thought of being content made me smile. I liked the idea of being happy *and* content.

A commotion in the middle of the group interrupted my reverie. "Snake! Snake! Snake," Raven screamed, "There's a snake!" Startled by the screams, her horse stomped, reared on its hind legs, and bolted. Prince Trueheart took off so quickly after Raven my head spun. Rhey hurriedly trotted up to Raven's vacant spot in the caravan. The other travelers stopped and looked around.

Dreadful high-pitched screeches split the air high above us. Fear struck our hearts as we looked up at the sky. Hideous creatures riding vultures fixed their bows and rained arrows down on us.

"*Run*! To the rocks—the snake's daimons are here!" Rhey forcefully commanded. I quickly dismounted Swift. "Everyone, leave your belongings. Men, bring your shields and *ruuunnnn*! Alli, if you still have your trumpet, now is the time to blow it!"

I grabbed my backpack in total panic. My hands were shaking so hard I fumbled with the latch. Dang! I struggled to get it open. "Calm down, Alli!" I mumbled under my breath. After a few moments, I finally opened my bag. Meanwhile, the kids cried as their mothers and fathers hauled them quickly toward the outcrop of rocks.

"Men, on my count, lift your shields. One, two, three!" Rhey counted loudly. The men held their shields together, providing a fort of protection for us from the raining arrows. I moved to the edge.

Rhey turned to me, "Now! Alli, blow!"

I took my trumpet out of its pouch. Could I even make a sound with my lips so dry? I had to! Oh, King! Help me! I wet my lips and tried to blow, but hardly any sound escaped. I tried again. Nope, nothing. *Come on, Alli. You gotta do better than this*, I urged. Okay! I took the deepest breath I could, licked my lips, and placed my mouth on the trumpet. I let go of a giant burst of air—a massive sound escaped from the trumpet. Wow! I never knew there was that much power inside me. I took another breath and blew the trumpet loudly again. I couldn't believe it. The sound confused the creatures above us. Screams and cries of agony filled the skies.

"Again, Alli, again!" Rhey ordered.

I took another deep breath, licked my lips, and blew the trumpet as hard as I could. Sounds of fighting surrounded our hiding place amongst the rocks; swords clashed and slashed. Rhey and the other men fought for us. I heard the echo of another trumpet, followed by the thundering of hooves. I peeked beyond the edge of the shields and saw an army of knights from the King's realm perched atop the most brilliantly white horses.

"Archers, ready your bows!" the commander yelled, "Now!"

Above the shields, we heard sounds of the victims of their aim falling from the sky. "Ahhhs" and thuds filled the air outside, but under our canopy of shields, there was a hush. Even the children quieted down. Then just like in my dreams, a bluish fog filled our hiding place. As we breathed in the fog, fear loosened its grip, and a calm settled over us.

I took a deep breath and remembered the roar of the lion; immediately, bravery replaced my fear. How was Raven doing? Was she safe? I didn't like the girl, but I didn't want anything bad to happen to her, especially at the hands of the snake.

The noise from the battle began dying down, so I snuck another peek through the edge of the shields. One of the knights was leading Raven toward me. She was whimpering and shaken up. "Here! See to her needs," he barked and turned on his steed.

"Are you all right?" I managed to ask. Raven's eyes were filled with fear. She stood silently in shock. "Come here," I said soothingly and reached for her hand. We gently clasped hands, and I drew her under the shelter.

"Sit here with me. I know how you feel. I have met the snake before. I know how scary he can be. It will be okay," I reassured her.

"Thanks," she sniffled. I reached into my pack and gave her a tissue to blow her nose. She sat there numbly while we waited.

Rhey rode over to us, "It's all right now. You can all come out. It is over. Is anyone hurt?"

One of the men stood at attention and replied, "Sir, miraculously, we have some scrapes and bruises but no serious injuries."

The men lifted their shields off the rocks. The fog was still present but not as thick as it had been. Prince Trueheart came galloping back on his unicorn, its horn glowing iridescent blue. They both looked as valiant as ever. The "battlefield," however, was shocking. There were no visible remnants of the battle. There were no fallen creatures, no birds, no arrows. Where were the remains of the battle?

Prince Trueheart announced, "Quickly as you can, ready yourselves. We need to hurry to the shelter prepared for us. Hurry! Now!"

We gathered ourselves and our belongings to continue the journey. The women and children were still in shock as they returned quietly to the path.

"Are you going to be okay?" I asked Raven.

"I think so," she managed to smile slightly. It seemed the bitterness was fading from her face; it was then that I noticed she was really pretty.

"Time to go, Alli," Rhey called.

I hurried over to Rhey. He reached down and lifted me onto Swift.

CAMPING

The numbness and shock from the battle wore off as we trudged forward, looking for a place to rest. The hours crawled by slowly, like the last day of school when it takes forever waiting for the final bell to ring to start summer break.

We finally arrived at our next stop. Everyone began setting up camp as Rhey and Prince Trueheart directed. The women prepared food while the children looked for wood to build fires. Tasked with fetching the water, I grabbed a bucket and made my way to the stream.

"Alli," Saraiyah suddenly appeared beside me at the stream. Wow! Would I ever get used to her surprise visits? She continued, "You are a brave girl. You did very well in the battle."

"Thank you, but I was so scared. I didn't feel very brave."

"Well, you know, bravery isn't the absence of fear, but rather pushing through in the face of fear. Being brave means facing things when it's the hardest."

"It just happened so fast. I didn't have time to think."

Saraiyah replied matter-of-factly, "Times of trouble is precisely the time when you see what is truly inside you. Rather than retreat, you chose to draw from the strength the King placed in you and rise to the call." She continued after taking a brief pause, "Now, I need to ask you to do something difficult. Will you do it for me?"

Hesitantly, I replied, "If I can."

Saraiyah smiled, "Things will be harder this time because you'll be able to think about it first. We need you to be a friend to Raven. She needs you, and in time, you may find you need her too. Would you be open to that?"

"I'm not sure. I've never had a friend. I don't even know how to." I was telling the truth. How would I know? I never went out of my way to make friends, especially someone I didn't even like.

Saraiyah looked at me with her bright shining eyes, "It's important, Alli. We wouldn't ask this of you if it wasn't."

"Okay. All I can do is try."

"You don't have to try. Only be open and willing to be her friend. I'll be there to help you do the impossible. It is like blowing your trumpet. You did not blow it all by yourself, right?"

"I don't know. I guess not," my voice wavered with uncertainty.

"Do you remember the King's roar and how brave you

felt afterward?"

"Yeah, of course. I don't think I would ever forget that moment."

"That's where your strength came from. Well, let me say this: the lion's roar watered the seeds of bravery in you. Remember when the King said, 'There is more inside of you than you realize.' Be encouraged: He was right. This journey will help bring out the real Alli. The Alli hidden inside of you is full of treasures. While here, you will begin to discover your true self. We are all very proud of you. Remember, I am with you, even when you cannot see me. I will be with you."

"Thank you," I barely whispered. I wanted to say something nice back, but I was too stunned by her words. As Saraiyah left, I thought about the things she had just said. Hidden treasures...Hmmm.

We sat quietly around the fire, everyone subdued by the day. Until unexpectedly, the lion made a surprise visit, calmly strolling from the forest. When Prince Boqer's paws hit the ground, a deep bass drumbeat vibrated, and colored light rippled out toward us. We felt better as each wave of light and sound reached us, bringing Him nearer. Like a cool rain falling on a hot summer day, His presence brought relief.

"Children," He announced, "you did well in your first battle together. You will face more battles. Success comes with being united to overcome the Dark Kingdom. There is power in unity." He paused and shifted His gaze toward me, "Alli, Raven, and I appreciate your demonstration of this today."

Raven bowed slightly and nodded in agreement with him. Prince Boqer continued, "Take courage! Remember: My Father, the Great King, and I will never leave you. You will never battle alone."

He left us with a "*Rrraaaaawwwrrrr!*" His roar vibrated and shook the ground beneath us. Majestically, He sauntered back into the forest. I could not take my eyes off Him. He was so *a-ma-zing*. I didn't know why, but I would give my life for Him. Well, maybe not my life, but at least, I'd give myself to His cause. At that moment, I knew for a fact I was different. While I was here and around Prince Boqer, things were changing in me. I liked it, and I didn't want it to stop.

After Prince Boqer left, Prince Trueheart, Rhey, and some from our group discussed plans by the fire. Prince Trueheart stood up, then called, "Everyone, may we have your attention, please?"

Once we gathered, he said, "You all did great in today's unforeseen attack. If everyone hadn't responded so well, the incident could have been disastrous. We need to be prepared for the enemy without giving him too much attention. He thrives on causing fear." Prince Trueheart's voice resonated with the travelers. Many nodded at the truth of his words.

"What are you proposing?" asked one of the newcomers.

"We will assign watchmen. We'll begin rotations in groups of four or five. Since the snake attacked the middle of our group, we will station watchmen throughout. All able twenty to sixty-year-olds will take shifts. However, please remember: everyone must be alert."

"What about me?" protested one of the new teenaged travelers. He and his widowed mother and younger brother had just joined us this morning. "I'm not twenty, but I'm strong and well-trained."

Rhey eyed him steadily and said, "Dylan, do you know how to shoot a bow?"

"Yes, Sir. My father died when I was eight. I became the man of the family."

"How old are you now, lad?" Rhey queried.

Dylan stood at attention, standing as tall as possible, "I am sixteen, Sir."

Rhey consulted quietly with Prince Trueheart. "Very well, then, Dylan. We will place your name on the list of watchmen. Everyone, please be aware of your surroundings. We will assign you partners. No one is to be alone."

Oh, joy! I thought unhappily, *A travel buddy.*

Rhey continued his instructions, "Report any concerns to us. You never know how the enemy may try to sneak in."

Prince Trueheart joined in the coaching, "All of you, including men, women, and children, will be warriors by the end of this journey. We need six volunteers to scout ahead of us while the rest of you secure the camp. Parents, please do not scare your children: teach them to be mindful of their surroundings and stay with the group. Everyone must do their part for us to complete the journey."

Rhey looked at me, "Alli, you and Raven are responsible for teaching the eight through ten-year-olds to avoid snakes." He shifted his gaze to one of the fathers. "Peter, will you escort them to find sticks for weapons? I don't want anyone walking about without one."

"Yes, of course, Sir," confirmed Peter.

"Dylan, go with them also," Rhey directed. Dylan nodded and smiled. He was pleased to have an important assignment.

Prince Trueheart dismissed everyone, "To your tasks, please."

I dreaded my task for many reasons, but mainly because I didn't want to be with Raven. As I pondered the task ahead, I let out a huge sigh. I promised Saraiyah I'd be willing to be her friend. So, I had to be willing. I had to keep my word. Upset, I quietly muttered, "All right, Ima, you better help me with this because I can't do this on my own."

"Did you say something to me, Alli?" Raven asked.

"Umm. No. I was just thinking out loud," I replied.

"Oh, I see. You know, they say if you answer yourself, that's when you know you're crazy."

"I didn't answer myself," I quipped defensively. A small smile crept across her lips, and I realized she was just teasing me. Great! She was one of those. *Okay, Ima,* I said in my mind, *I'm willing to be willing, but I need your help to do even that.* Then I shifted focus to the assigned task.

As we gathered sticks with Peter and Dylan, Raven rambled on and on about her life. She talked about her family and home, struggles at school, and even her secret boy crush. She also spoke about music and a bunch of stuff I wasn't interested in. I wanted to tune her out, but I made a promise, so I chose to pay attention. I needed to listen to be a good friend. After I listened to her for a few more minutes, I realized she wasn't that bad after all.

Later, after the group shared a delicious dinner around the fire, Prince Trueheart pulled out a book.

"Let us end our night by reading from the King's Chronicles."

He held a copy of the same book Saraiyah had given me. I wondered how he would read the book to us because reading this book required eating the book. Prince Trueheart tore out a page from the book and handed a fragment to each traveler. I watched as he gave each person a piece, but the page never changed. A sigh of wonder escaped my lips. In a moment, he was handing me my fragment of the page. I placed the piece in my mouth, and just like the last time, a beautiful scene opened right before my eyes. The only difference was the narrator: Prince Trueheart's voice filled my head this time.

When the scene had finished playing, Prince Trueheart stopped speaking. I yawned sleepily and readied for bed. The mothers gathered their children, the travelers prepared for rest, and the leaders instructed the watchmen. As the day unwound to its end, I breathed a sigh of relief. At least, I knew we would be safe for the night.

SHOOTING LESSONS

"Good morning, Miss Alli! I want to show you something," Rhey called over to me as I ate breakfast, "Finish your breakfast and meet me over there." He pointed toward the creek.

"Okay!" I said with a nod. I usually take my time eating, but I quickly finished breakfast and headed toward the creek. A groan escaped my lips when I was just a few yards from where Rhey was waiting for me.

"Oh no! Are you kidding me?" I objected under my breath. Raven was sitting on a stump waiting there too. Rhey must have invited us both to the creek. Was she to be my partner? As I drew close to them, I decided to make the best of it and forced myself to smile.

"Ready, Miladies? Let's go!" Rhey eagerly jumped into action and led us down the small footpath to a clearing. As we ducked under the last few trees, I saw a target hanging on a tree trunk. Before I could process what we were doing there, Rhey interrupted my thoughts, "Today, you will learn to shoot a bow."

Raven and I exchanged a quick glance but stood quietly, discomfort written on both of our faces.

"Miladies, the Great King wants you equipped for battle. These are the weapons He's chosen for you. They will go in your packs." I started to ask how they would fit but stopped myself, as I knew, somehow, they just would.

"Miss Alli," he continued, "here is your bow. Her name is Morning Song."

Rhey handed me a beautiful silver bow with ornate etching. The handle was the profile of a woman's face, with the grip silhouetting around the face's curves. The bow looked more like a work of art than a weapon. I didn't know anything about fine craftsmanship, but I was pretty sure this was a shining example.

"Here is your bow, Miss Raven. His name is Night Wind," Rhey said smiling as he handed Raven an exotic-looking chestnut-colored wooden bow. Her grip was a man's silhouette. Her bow, like mine, had beautifully detailed carvings and looked like a piece of art also.

Rhey immediately started our lesson. He told us how to care for, how to hold, and how to shoot our bows. His knowledge and confidence helped relieve some of my concerns about learning to shoot a bow. That was until he called my name first to begin target practice.

"All right, Miss Alli, let's begin with you."

I hesitated a bit, then picked up my bow. It was much lighter than I expected. Once in my hands, it felt very natural. I lifted the bow, held it as Rhey had instructed, and looked at my target. *Okay, you can do this*, I assured myself. I carefully notched my arrow, pulled my bowstring back by my face, and let it fly. My arrow shot straight to the heart of the circle: a perfect bullseye! I stood in quiet disbelief. Did I just make a bullseye on my first shot?

"Good one, Milady!" Rhey beamed, "Now, Miss Raven, you have a go."

Raven hit a perfect bullseye too. We looked at each other in amazement.

"Again, please," Rhey insisted.

Raven and I continued alternating shots, each time hitting the bullseye. It seemed like we couldn't miss the bullseye...that was until...I shifted my hand position ever so slightly on my bow grip. When I shot the next arrow, not only did I miss the mark, but my arrow went soaring through the trees. I looked at Rhey, confused.

"Miss Alli, you accidentally covered the eyes of the lady of the bow in your bow grip. You cannot cover her eyes; you won't hit your mark."

Ooh! The bow was making the bullseye! It had nothing to do with me. I chuckled to myself. I was just lucky enough to be chosen to hold the bow. Raven realized this at the same time. We both looked at our bows, looked at each other, made a funny face, and just started laughing and laughing.

"That was really something, wasn't it?" Raven asked as we made our way back to camp.

"Boy, I'll say," I admitted, "I've done things on this journey I never imagined I would do in my whole life."

"Yeah, me too! Honestly, Alli," she said sheepishly, "If I'm being completely real, I didn't like you very much when I first met you. You seemed a bit standoffish, not very nice. But the more I get to know you, the more I like you. I think you're cool. Actually, you are pretty fun!" She teased with a funny face. "By the way, thanks for the other day. I don't know what I would have done if you hadn't been there for me, after the snake and all."

"Uh, you're welcome. I didn't do much."

Raven's face got serious, and she lowered her eyes, "You were a great comfort to me, more than you know."

"I'm glad I could help," I squeaked out. The weight of her honesty and gratitude caused me to continue. "Um," I hesitated, "since we are being completely honest, I…uh… have to admit I didn't like you very much either. I thought you were mean. You looked so angry all the time."

"Oh, that!" Raven chuckled, "Yeah, I look like that when I'm kinda scared."

"Well, I guess you must've been more than kinda scared," I teased with a giggle. We both laughed, shedding our discomfort with each other.

"Actually, I was petrified. I don't do well in large crowds," she admitted.

"Really?" My eyes widened, "*Me either!*"

All the sharing between Raven and me had my thoughts swirling. Was it like this with everyone? Were people so different on the inside from the outside? After all, Raven was nothing I expected. I thought she was mean, stingy, spoiled, but she was just scared...like me. We felt the same way but showed it differently. As I realized we were more alike than I had ever imagined, a smile came across my lips. Were we becoming friends?

Just then, Raven interrupted my thoughts. "Race ya back!" she shouted and took off running.

"Wait!" I shouted and sped up to chase her. She was running so fast there was no chance of catching her. Finally, she stopped at the creek where the day's adventure began. Raven dropped to the ground, laughing and smiling at me. I sat beside her to catch my breath. No one said anything funny, but we couldn't stop laughing. On and on, we howled with laughter.

"That wasn't fair!" I said indignantly when I caught my breath. Raven just smiled.

DISCOVERY

I looked at Raven and saw her in a whole new light as if I was seeing her for the first time. The twisting of her face was gone; she looked so pretty. Even her voice was sweet now. I finally saw the real Raven, the Raven before life hardened and changed her.

"Raven, what happened when the snake took you? You've been so different since then."

She breathed in deeply and then slowly let it out. "Yeah, I guess that's probably true. The snake incident was the worst thing that ever happened to me. I was so scared. Alli, I thought I was going to die. The snake tried to drag me down into a very dark hole. I thought he was going to eat me alive. My life changed in an instant. When I thought it was all over, I realized how good life really was and how much I wanted to live. All I could do was whimper. I felt hopeless, but then I remembered the Great King. Just the thought of Him gave me a spark of hope, so I said a little prayer, asking for help. Right after that, Prince Trueheart showed up and rescued me. I was so relieved and grateful.

He led me to the knight who returned me to the shelter, and everyone was so nice. You were there, and you were so kind to me. Having you all there was so helpful to me.

"After the battle ended, Saraiyah talked to me about my life and my previous troubles. She said I didn't have to let the hurts from my past steal the life from my todays. She showed me how my bitterness enabled the snake to grab me. I was holding on to the past instead of letting it go. Bitterness was having its way in me, rather than love and forgiveness."

"Really?" I asked. "Wow."

Raven continued, "Yeah." She slowly exhaled.

Seeing the tears glistening in her eyes, I waited, knowing she needed a minute.

"Saraiyah had me make a little pile of twigs to represent all the bad things I was holding on to. As I placed each twig on the pile, Saraiyah helped me forgive each person for the hurt they caused. I even cried a little bit while we did it," she confessed.

"When I placed the last twig on the pile, I looked up and discovered the lamb, you know, Sir Reynald? He had joined us, but he was dressed so differently. It was the strangest thing. He wore a bloodred sash over bright white clothes. He watched intently as Saraiyah and I burned my pile of twigs. The smoke from my little pile rose into the air, and tears spilled down my cheeks. I looked at Sir Reynald, and he was quietly crying too. His tears were spilling down his face into the flames. We watched until the pile burned up and disappeared. When it was over, Sir Reynald looked at me and told me he was very sorry about the bad things that happened to me. He said he could help me heal from all the old heartaches if I would allow him. He asked if I wanted him to help me, and I said yes. Then he touched my shoulder, and I really cried." As Raven paused, her eyes were shining like two beautiful sapphires. "I bawled like a baby, she admitted. All the hurt inside left like water down the drain. Then, you know what happened next?"

"What?" I asked, fascinated by her story.

"Sir Reynald, that beautiful lamb, reached down to where the fire had been and picked up a little black obsidian-like rock. He handed it to me and said, 'Raven, this rock formed from our tears mingled together in the fire. Keep this treasure to remind you of today: the day you joined life again.' And he was right. I started to live again, and I've felt different ever since."

"Wow!" My eyes grew big as I stared at Raven, taking in all the details of her story. It was hard to believe the incredible things I had just heard. "Thank you so much for sharing your story with me. It was beautiful."

"Thanks for listening," she said with a sweet smile.

"Sure thing! We better rejoin the group; we don't want to miss dinner!" I said, grinning. We laughed and headed back toward the center of camp.

Later that night, as I reflected on my time with Raven, I realized some great things about life. Raven was not the only person who changed since this journey began. I changed too. Friendship was not some magical thing that only lucky people found. It happened as people took a chance and shared their hearts. You had to be open with friends and let them see the real you, which is probably why I always hid from friendships. I was afraid no one would like what they saw if they got too close. The thought of people getting close to me still made me uncomfortable. Just then, like a whisper in the wind, I heard, "Trust the goodness of the King." The phrase settled my fears. My habit of avoiding people wasn't working out for me. I had no friends. I needed to keep my promise to Saraiyah. Be open. Be willing. It was my only hope of having a real friend.

COMMUNITY

It was morning; we were back on the trail, and the landscape was changing. As we moved further away from camp, valleys looked deeper and narrower; trees seemed smaller. Although the path didn't feel much like an incline, we were climbing. Looming in front of us was an extremely tall cliff face. I didn't see any path or trail. Questions flooded my mind as we drew closer to King's Mountain. How would we ever get up that mountainside? Would we rock climb? Was there some sort of ride to take us to the top? We would arrive sooner than we thought.

I reasoned with myself, *Forget about the uncertainty of traveling the mountain and focus on the present, Alli! What new weird or cool things would we see?* Out of the blue, a wave of homesickness hit me. *You can't get sad around all these people. Pull it together! Focus on the group.* My eyes wandered the crowd, and I noticed a few unfamiliar faces. Was it my imagination, or had more people joined us? Rhey must've picked up more invitees. I shrugged, thinking, *The more, the merrier.* Wow! Did I just think *the more, the merrier*? The growing crowd didn't really bother me much this time. I sighed, ignored the homesick feelings, and watched the ground before me.

Raven and I walked with the group of eight- to ten-year-olds assigned to us. We were teaching them to avoid snakes. I didn't have a clue how to teach them about snakes, but Raven was a natural. She took the lead by showing them where to walk and how to watch the path. She told them, "Always stay on the path, avoid tall grass, and never run ahead. Snakes can hurt you; this is not a game. And if you see one, do *not* pick it up!"

I was very impressed with her patience and teaching ability. Watching her with the children, however, made me glad I was an only child. The thought of my mom having more kids made me chuckle. Thank goodness I didn't have a bunch of siblings running around; I did *not* have the patience for them.

The sun was high in the sky when we stopped at one of the King's gazebos. Everything for a fun and restful day was right there like the other rest areas. Tall trees and fragrant flowers surrounded the clearing, while a small, babbling brook with crisp, clear water ran through the center. Bright-colored birds flitted from bush to bush, and chattering squirrels chased each other from tree to tree. Curious little chipmunks ran up to the travelers' bags looking for treats. A deer coaxed her baby fawn to drink from the brook, and the rabbit moms hurried their rabbit babies into their dens. The whole scene was alive with wonder. Beauty was everywhere I looked. Oh, wait! What was that? A kangaroo? I burst into laughter. The King must've thrown him in just to keep us on our toes.

The kids ran straight to the brightly colored playground. Boy, I knew they were glad to see that! They played knights and dragons, lords and ladies, hide and seek. I even heard a few children from our group playing "cut the head off the snake." Way to go! I was really happy about that game. Although I wasn't really a "kid person," they were fun to watch. Their imagination and enthusiasm were inspiring. I was even a bit concerned for them, making sure the little kids didn't go near the brook. Honestly, they were so busy with the playground they didn't even seem to notice the water, but I stood nearby with a watchful eye…just in case.

Out of thin air, servants appeared with piles of delicious foods on elaborate trays. There were sweet fruits, pastries, cakes, cookies, and every good thing you could imagine. Even the children left playing and came running when they smelled the delicious meal. All of this reminded me of my welcome feast. The only thing missing was Sir Reynald.

At the end of our meal, Rhey stood on a bench and called, "Everyone, let's have a time of thanksgiving to our King. Giving thanks not only honors our King but encourages us as well. As we share, may you be refreshed and filled with gratitude."

The voices of fellow travelers popped up here and there from the crowd; their stories and gratitude made everyone happy. I felt encouraged and inspired by their stories. The funniest thing happened: the air filled with the sweetest smell, lavender mixed with summer rain.

After most people shared something, we wrote a personal message to thank our beloved King. Each traveler signed the message, and Rhey rolled the paper into a tiny little scroll. A beautiful bluebird swooped down and landed on the long table, waiting patiently as Prince Trueheart attached the little scroll to her leg. Then with a chirp and a flutter, she flew off to the King's castle.

As we headed out to the path in the morning, I was recharged and well-rested. I felt great! Being with the other travelers *was* like some kind of superfood for me. Maybe Saraiyah was right about all the togetherness stuff. Was Saraiyah near us in her invisible way? It certainly seemed like it.

The awkwardness that once slowed Raven's and my conversations was gone; we laughed and chattered like we had known each other our whole lives. Before I knew it, I told her things I hadn't told anyone…personal stuff. I was surprised when the words left my mouth. I trusted her, and she seemed to trust me because she told me personal stuff. Why was I telling her all my secrets? That's when I realized we were really becoming friends. My face beamed as the truth hit me, *I have a friend!* "I don't see any flat areas to set up camp," I said to Raven as the sun dipped behind the enormous mountains. "We will need a place to rest for the night. I hope Rhey and Prince Trueheart know where they are taking us."

"Yeah, I hope so too. I don't want to have to sleep standing up!" Raven chuckled.

We laughed at that. Raven's whole face lit up when she smiled. How different she looked now! I couldn't help but notice again how beautiful she was.

Thankfully, after we rounded the next corner, we saw a few caves up ahead, and the timing couldn't have been better. The wind picked up speed, the sky darkened, and thunder rumbled loudly in the distance. Everyone scurried for the caves to avoid being caught in the storm. We had barely gotten into the cave when a massive bolt of lightning cracked outside, rumbling the ground under our feet. Whew! We made it.

The cave was so dark we couldn't see anything. Thankfully, Rhey lit a torch as soon as we entered the cave. When my eyes adjusted to the light, I saw a vast open area in the cave. Prince Trueheart lit torches mounted on the cave walls; light immediately filled the room and spilled down the corridors. A few men and teens led the horses and pack animals to an adjoining cave, making the main room less crowded. The flickering torchlight added just enough light to be comfortable. Interestingly, the torches were prepped and ready for our arrival. *All your needs will be met.* All your needs…indeed, those words included every last detail.

With the torches lit, the moms made dinner. Raven and I gathered some of the kids to play games and keep them out of the adult's hair. Honestly, it was fun. Playing with the children certainly helped us forget about the storm outside. At least for a while, anyway.

NIGHT TERRORS

Thankfully, the men were on full alert because, in the middle of the night, the enemy tried to get into the cave. We awoke to the watchmen's cries, "Awake! Awake! We're under attack." Pandemonium broke out: the children started crying; their mothers comforted them, and the men grabbed their weapons.

What should I do? Run? Hide? Go deeper into the cave? I didn't know what to do, so I just stupidly sat, waiting for instructions. It felt like forever but was only a few seconds.

"Everyone, grab what you can! Bring your weapons!" Rhey yelled.

"Children, get your snake sticks!" I called. My little charges had laid them nearby and quickly grabbed them.

"Peter, have your bravest men block the entrance to the cave! You and your sons protect the women and children! Eli, Samson, Benjamin," Rhey barked, "bring your teams to the frontline with Trueheart. Hurry everyone, let's go!"

After firing off his instructions, Rhey set a furious pace

taking the rest of us deeper into the cave. Despite the torches, the darkness was thick, so thick I couldn't see my own hand in front of my face. When Rhey disappeared around a bend, his torch left only a small reflection dancing on the cave walls.

"Be alert!" Rhey cried, his voice echoing back to us. "The enemy may have set traps along here." Down, down, down we went. The passageway turned around and around, feeling endless. My throat was so dry I could hardly swallow. Sounds of fighting bounced off the cave walls. The men ahead of us were battling who knows what. The cave grew colder, and the passageways became smaller the further down we went. Oh no! Were those gleaming red eyes above and below? My heart was racing. Were there terrible snakes and creatures hiding in wait to take us captive? I couldn't give in to my fear. I had to move quickly to keep up with the group.

Suddenly, the narrow passageway opened slightly on the back of the cave. As we neared the opening, I heard rushing water. Stretched out in front of us was a very long wooden footbridge. It was so dark, and the bridge was so long that I couldn't see to the end. But it was the only way to the other side. I didn't know how high the bridge was, but I knew falling was not an option. If the fall didn't get you, the rushing water would! All of this added to my fear.

"Help me, my King! Where are You?"

The words scarcely left my lips when I remembered my trumpet. I fumbled with my bag and pulled it out. Putting it to my mouth, I tried to blow. Nothing—no sound, just like the last time I tried to play it. *Okay, take your time! You can do this,* I calmed myself down and attempted again, this time with a big breath of air. The trumpet barely made a sound. I didn't have time to worry about it. We were pressed to get across the bridge. Panic was rising as the sounds of fighting got louder and louder ahead of us, coming from the end of the bridge.

Raven and I moved slowly, bringing the children with us. They were crying and needed reassurance. "Shhhh! Little ones, it will be all right. Remember," I encouraged, "the King loves us." We coaxed them to move across the seemingly endless footbridge as quickly as possible.

Next, to my horror, someone fell off the bridge. I heard a cry and a splash as they hit the water. Then, I heard a sizzling sound, like a hot frying pan set in cold water. *What a relief!* I thought. *It must have been one of the snake's daimons.* They were the foul creatures who rode the vultures in the first battle. More and more daimons fell from the bridge: screaming, splashing, sizzling. Could it be the result of blowing my trumpet?

"Hurry, everyone! We are almost there!" someone cried out.

"Alli, do you think we are going to be okay?" Raven asked, her eyes as big as saucers.

"Yeah. Su…Sure," I stuttered. At this point, I was trembling pretty much uncontrollably. I just could *not* stop shaking.

"Hurry, children! Hurry!" I said more boldly. Raven and

I picked up the youngest children and grabbed the hands of some others. Everyone held on to someone, staying connected. Finally, after what seemed like an eternity, we reached the end of the bridge. I wanted to whoop out loud because we made it to the other side! Relief washed over me. It only lasted a few moments, though. There were two corridors at the end of the bridge: two ways to go. Somehow, we had gotten separated from our leaders. None of us knew which passage to take. *Do we go left or right?* we wondered. We were numb.

At last, Dylan spoke up, "Let's wait, everyone. Shhh! Listen closely."

We heard voices echoing in the distance but couldn't tell where they were coming from. The walls felt alive, absorbing and distorting the sounds. Were the walls fighting us? Or maybe it was those red-eyed daimon things? We had no idea where the men had gone; one moment, they led the mothers and babies, and the next moment, they were gone! We were alone! The thought panicked me. What were we going to do now?

The children began whimpering. "Quiet!" hissed Tom, or Thomas, one of the teens who recently joined our group. "We can't hear!" he sneered at the kids.

Tom bugged me, but I decided not to judge him too fast after what I'd learned with Raven.

"Look, I know we are all scared, but let's try to keep our cool. Maybe our leaders went this way," I pointed to my right. "Come on, let's go! If I'm wrong, we can just come back here. Okay?" I charged ahead. I didn't know what came over me, but I couldn't stop, even if I wanted to. I took the lead and yelled, "Hey, Raven. You bring up the rear and keep those kids calm. We must trust the Great King!"

Everyone fell in line behind me and headed to the right, with me leading in the front. The sound of the men's voices was getting fainter, but I felt like we had found the right tunnel. The passageway was dim; we had only one torch left; the others had been dropped in the panic or gone out. As we moved forward, the tunnel began to incline. I hoped we were moving toward the surface. At least we weren't going down anymore. I was already feeling better about my choice to go to the right.

Abruptly, the passage widened to an open area with no exit. The light from the torch barely lit the darkness of the cave. "Okay, everyone. Gather round. Raven, where are you?" I called out to her.

"I'm right here. Bringing up the rear, as you ordered," she saluted me with a grin.

"Okay. Great," I chuckled with relief, grateful for Raven's sense of humor. "Dylan, can you take a quick headcount, please?"

"Of course," he obliged, "Mistress, there are twelve of us, six teens and six children."

I surveyed the walls of the cave. "All right. Let's check the walls to make sure we aren't missing a hidden exit or some kinda door."

"How are we supposed to do that? Do you think we read

braille or something?" Tom said sarcastically.

"Okay. Okay. I know it's hard, but we gotta work together if we want to get out of here," I said convincingly. "You guys check the walls to my left, and you guys check the walls to my right. Raven, stay here with me. We gotta calm these kids!"

The children sniveled and fussed as we tried to quiet them.

"Hush! Hush! Listen!" I encouraged them and placed my finger in front of my lips. The children's eyes were wide with fear. After a few moments, we heard low voices murmuring from inside the cave. It was odd to listen to them and not know where they were coming from.

I announced, "We are children of the King, and He has promised never to leave us. I know all of this is scary. I'm scared too. We gotta stick together and trust the Great King. He will take care of us. Andrew, how many weapons do we have? I have my bow. Children, do you have your snake sticks?" The children nodded their assent. "Okay. Great! Now be brave. We will get through this if we stick together!"

"Who died and made *you* boss?" Tom complained.

I ignored his comment. I didn't have time for fear disguised as sarcasm.

No one found anything on the cave walls: no hidden exits or secret passageways.

I prayed out loud, "Dear King, we need Your help.

Please, come." Just as I finished my plea, I remembered my trumpet again. I pulled it from my backpack and pursed my lips. I blew as hard as I could. Suddenly, beautiful, powerful sounds came out of the trumpet as if it was alive. I played notes I'd never heard before. The sound reminded me of a cavalry call in the movies. It was amazing!

"Everyone, hearts and weapons ready!" Raven encouraged.

"Look!" Ryan, one of the little ones, exclaimed. He pointed his tiny finger toward a barely visible crack of light. The light grew brighter, piercing through the darkness and our fear.

"Alli! Blow your trumpet again! Hurry!" Dylan exclaimed.

I lifted my trumpet, took a huge breath, and blew as hard as I could. The crack got wider, and we excitedly moved closer to the light.

"Again! Alli! Again!" they cheered.

I blew my trumpet again and again. Each blast made the light-filled crevice larger and wider. Soon, the crack was big enough to fit through. We hurriedly bustled the children through the hole. Just before I stepped through, I looked back for Raven.

"Come on, Raven! Let's get outta here!" I grabbed her hand, and we climbed through to the other side—together.

NEW LEADERSHIP

"What has gotten into you?" Raven whispered.

"Honestly, I don't know!" I shrugged.

"Well, whatever it is, don't stop! I like it!" she chuckled, "Just try not to be so bossy. Okay?"

Bossy? I could not imagine someone calling me "bossy." In the past, I could barely look people in the eye or talk to strangers. I was happy being invisible. But now, I was taking charge, leading the group, and handing out orders. What had gotten into me?

After a short walk, we rounded a bend, and we were out of the oppressive cave! Everyone's explosive excitement filled the air. The sun shone brightly, birds sang, and the air smelled of sweet fragrances. We saw a stream a few yards away. We ran over to drink from it. Our parched throats welcomed the cool water. Raven and I gently washed the children's faces and small hands, dirtied from the cave.

Nearby was a huge bush with berries. I wondered if they were part of the King's provisions for us. "Who wants to go check out those berries and see if they are any good?" I said, trying not to be too bossy.

"I will," Andrew volunteered. "I was a King's scout!" he proudly proclaimed.

"You were? That's cool," I encouraged. "Dylan, can you go with him?"

"Sure thing! I'll be glad to," Dylan responded. What a relief! One task down! I watched the boys head toward the bush and then looked back at the children; their frightened little faces concerned me. I wanted to comfort them.

"Is anyone hurt?" I said, kneeling to their level. I shot a quick "help me" glance at Raven.

"Come on, children. Who wants to play a game?" The kids eagerly gathered around Raven, forgetting the ordeal within moments. They frolicked and played, just like they did before the cave.

A few minutes later, Dylan and Andrew arrived with handfuls of berries. "They seem to be edible and most delicious," reported Andrew.

"Hey, guys! Let's eat!" Dylan shouted. The children gathered around him as he walked to the stream. We sat to enjoy our delicious and most-welcomed meal.

"Where did the others go?" Raven asked. "Do you think we will meet up with our leaders?"

"I don't know, but in case we don't, who will lead us? How will we find our way to the King's castle?" Dylan asked. "Leading seemed to come naturally to you," he said, looking at me.

I looked beside me to see if he was talking to someone else because I knew he could not be talking to me. "M…m… me?" I stuttered. "No way! Not me. I can't lead."

Is he accusing me? I was a little bothered by his suggestion. I was *not* a leader!

"Okay, let's vote," Raven interrupted my self-talk, quickly diffusing the situation. "Let's vote to see who should lead us to the castle. Then we can all agree and make it together. Group effort!" she encouraged.

"What would the King, Saraiyah, and Rhey do?" I wondered aloud.

Just then, Prince Boqer arrived, right in the middle of us! We were startled to the core but completely relieved. The children let out shrill cries of joy when they saw Him. Thrilled, they headed straight for Him. He chuckled as they crowded around Him, hugging His legs.

"Gather round, My children; this is a secret place." His breath was like a gentle breeze that blew away all our fear. "Here, you are under My protection. The snake and his daimons cannot bother you. Go ahead, set up camp, and rest here for the night."

"Alli!" Saraiyah's voice grabbed my attention, and I spun around, desperate to see her. There she was. I ran into her outstretched arms, excited to see her. "I am so very proud of you," she whispered as she welcomed my hug. "You have done so well!"

Stunned by her words of affirmation, I drew back just enough to see her face. Her eyes were like oceans of liquid love. Relief filled me as I leaned into her wonderful hug. She held me and let the fear and stress of the day drain from me. After a few moments, I moved back again, looking at her.

"All better?" Her eyes twinkled with joy. I nodded yes. "Wonderful! Come with me, dear girl."

Saraiyah took my hand and led me to the edge of a very tall cliff. The view was breathtaking. Below us was the path we had been traveling. Taking in the sights, I could see all the way back to the beginning of my journey.

"Look, there!" she directed me to look behind us, to the castle; it was so grand nothing else could fit in my view. It dominated the landscape.

"Alli, we want you to see how far you have come and remind you of your destination. This is our gift to you. Remember this as you continue your journey. Sometimes, it's hard to keep perspective about these things. As you recall this scene, you will see we have been with you all along. This will give you the confidence to push through when things are difficult. No matter what you see or feel, we are always with you." Her words rang through me. "Now, don't you have some folks waiting on you? Time to scoot! Remember, no matter what you face, look for a way of escape. We will show you the way if you only trust."

As I walked back to camp, I thought about everything since my invitation arrived. Of all the things I had seen, I was amazed most by the changes in me. The fearful observer was leaving, and in her place was an emerging, strong, confident leader. Could I be a strong, confident leader? Would my mom even recognize me when I got home? For the first time since I had gotten here, I was fully aware of my previous life. I had been so immersed in the adventure I rarely thought of home. I knew things would never be the same. The refreshing of Saraiyah's visit stayed with me and gave me clarity. Although I didn't know what was coming next, I knew I was ready for it.

I felt tapping on my shoulder; it was a stick, and Dylan was on the other end of it.

"Miss Alli, are you awake?" Dylan said.

"Hmm. What? Huh?" Groggily, I realized I had been dreaming. I yawned and tried to shake off sleep to answer him. My mind raced for a minute. I looked around and saw everyone else was napping. *What is going on? Were those berries poisonous?* As my thoughts cleared, I realized we must have fallen asleep after our meal. I sensed the rest was a gift from the King. Plus, we were roused by a fearful invasion in the night.

"Miss Alli," Dylan persisted, "do you think it's time we move on?"

"Yes, yes. Let's awaken the others," I responded. As I sat up and finished collecting my thoughts, I noticed Dylan's new alertness: new confidence in his face.

Once everyone was awake, we gathered around. I told everybody my dream of the lion's visit and Saraiyah's walk to the cliff. I shared Saraiyah's cliff message, hoping it would encourage them as much as it did me. After speaking with the group, Dylan, Raven, and I decided that this spot was safe and we could rest for the night.

Before going back to bed, we needed to finish the business of earlier: electing a leader. As Raven suggested, we took a vote. Although it was not unanimous, it was decided the leaders would be Dylan, Raven, and me. Tom disagreed, of course, but the vote stood. So, the following morning, after breakfast, we, the novice leaders, sat together and planned the next steps.

"Guys, I think we should get going before the snake and his daimons decide to come after us. Since we are going to the castle, we could head north to look for the path. How does that sound?" Dylan asked.

Raven and I agreed with Dylan. His plan was sound, so we prepared for the journey. Dylan counted the supplies we managed to get out of the cave. We had bota bags (leather canteens), weapons, dried fish, fruit, and a few hard biscuits. There weren't many supplies left, but I remembered the promise, "The King will supply all your needs." I reminded the group as we readied to resume our adventure. Our King's words reassured us. We finished packing, collected everyone, and set out.

Shortly after starting, we trekked up a hill with a curtain of vines at the top. As we approached, the vines opened as if to extend a little welcome to us. Behind the veil of vines was a well-marked path that wound into the mountains. The vines and path seemed to be showing us the way. Would we rejoin our leaders? Did this path hold some new kind of test, set up by the King?

We hopped onto the path and headed into the mountains. Before long, we heard the trickling of a stream; although hidden by the trees, the sound seemed to come from our right. Dylan and Andrew volunteered to check it out while the rest of us kept moving forward. We hiked on the path, which wove in and out of trees. Sunlight flickered through the overhead canopy of leaves. An atmosphere of adventure had invaded our little band of travelers as if we were on a treasure hunt. The foreboding weariness, like a dog nipping at our heels, was gone. Excitement filled the air. The children played lighthearted games along the way.

Soon, Dylan and Andrew rejoined us. "As far as we can tell, the stream looks clean and clear. We will have a fresh supply of water while we are close; if the path leads away from the water, we will have to fill our botas," Dylan said confidently.

"That is great, you guys! Let's keep our eyes peeled for anything we can use on our journey," Raven suggested.

"Sounds like a plan!" I said with enthusiasm.

The light faded as we trekked up the mountainside. Where would we set up camp for the night? Just then, I noticed a circular outcropping of rocks on our right. I drew the group's attention to the clearing. We headed over to investigate and found a small table with a basket and a pitcher. The basket was made of reeds and looked hand-made in that the pattern was uniquely beautiful but not perfect. Inside the basket, wrapped in white muslin, were a few small loaves of bread. The pitcher looked like something right out of Arabian tales; it rose above the table with a slender, tapered neck and a bellowing wide belly with ornately carved feet on the base. The pour spout curved along the side of the body before curving out at the top for the sake of pouring. The water inside was crystal clear and refreshing. The whole scene was a welcome sight for our band of travelers.

As grateful as I was to see the provisions, I couldn't help but question how the small amount of bread would fill all the empty bellies. *Certainly, the children will have to eat first, then...*I interrupted myself and mumbled under my breath, "Ima, we need more than this if we are gonna feed all these mouths."

Then, quietly in my mind, I heard, "Trust the goodness of the King," and I knew we were going to be okay. I didn't know how, but I just did.

"Hey, this looks like a great place to stop for the night," Dylan stated.

"Sounds good to me," I returned my vote, as did Raven. We all agreed and began setting up camp. The children were settling their blankets from their packs when Raven randomly burst into song:

"I will celebrate the goodness of our King,

He is the Great One and ruler of everything.

I know I am hidden safe within His care.

Come and lift your voice with me

As we celebrate the goodness of our King."

Andrew sang the second verse along with Raven, and soon, we were all singing.

Dylan offered a blessing at the end of our song. "Thank You, O Great King, for taking care of us along our path. We bless this bread and beverage."

Andrew went over to the small table, picked up the basket, and passed it around. As we took our bread from the basket, Dylan poured water into our makeshift cups from the pitcher. The water was purplish and sparkled like liquid diamonds. Honestly, it didn't look much like water but refreshed with every single sip. The bread had an airy texture and a slight taste of honey. We laughed, ate, and drank to our bellies' content. The basket and the pitcher never went empty; our King had, once again, provided for us.

We slept peacefully under the stars that night. Our bellies were full, and our minds were at ease. We knew we were safe under the protection and provision of the Great King.

LOST OUR WAY

The higher we climbed up the mountain, the lower our mood became. The climate within our group had shifted from excitement and adventure to boredom and struggle. We went from "Woo-hoo!" to "Where's the end?" We traveled for days since the cave, and the path was getting harder and narrower. We were relieved we hadn't seen the enemy but were a little on edge since the guys shared legends of the Dark Wilderness around the campfire. Occasionally, we heard a few scary sounds or saw red glints deep within the forest, but nothing significant. Honestly, I thought our biggest enemy was not the daimons but the relentless monotony! And the fear of not knowing when or *if* we would arrive. After all, we didn't even know if we were going the right way.

"Alli, do you think we're going to make it all the way up the mountain with these kids?" Tom whispered over my shoulder, "I mean, you know, they are great and all, but I've heard the mountain gets dangerous the higher you go. If the path gets more treacherous, I don't know if we can survive."

171

Surprised by his concern and caught a little off guard, I replied, "Next stop, let's discuss it with Raven and Dylan. Okay?"

"As you wish, oh mighty leader," he said and stiffly bowed.

I didn't know what got into him; he grew meaner by the day. However, now wasn't the time to give him much thought. The rocky terrain was getting more difficult to traverse. The path had narrowed and steepened, making the climb even more demanding. Earlier in the day, Godfrey, one of the youngest boys, stumbled and nearly fell off the hundred-foot cliff. Thankfully, Andrew grabbed him by the pants to keep him from tumbling over the side; but since that scare, the girls had grown weary and whiny while the boys grumbled and fought. I did not have to be a rocket scientist to figure out: our group was a mess...our trip was becoming a nightmare!

"Okay, this has got to stop," I mumbled under my breath. "Dylan!" I called to the front. "As soon as you see a good place, can we take a break?"

"Sure thing!" Dylan shouted back to me. "I see a spot up ahead. It is only a log and a few rocks, but at least we can sit."

"Great!" I muttered. But it wasn't great, though. I was tired and felt alone. I worried about where our leaders had gone. What if something terrible happened to them? What were we going to do?

"Why don't we focus our hearts on the Great King, and

then maybe we will know what to do," Raven suggested as we gathered in the new rest stop. I faintly smelled a hint of Saraiyah's fragrance. I breathed it in deeply and then sighed with relief.

"I've heard people say, when you get lost, you should return to the last place you knew where you were and then start again," Dylan said. "Maybe we should return to the cave." Although Dylan's reasoning made absolutely no sense to me, Raven and the others agreed with him. They thought it best to return to the cave. I did not think it was a good idea, but the other leaders had decided. We rested and set out the next day in the direction we had just come from.

Surprised and thankful, I rejoiced that the journey back to the cave took much less time than I expected: rather than several days, our return only took a few.

"We're getting close. Do you think we should send someone ahead to check it out?" Dylan asked.

"Wow! Great idea, Dylan!" I agreed.

"Andrew, do you want to come with me?" Dylan implored.

"Sure thing!" Andrew agreed, and the two journeyed on ahead.

"Come on! Let's wait over here while the guys go check everything out," Raven piped up.

Hours passed with no sign of Dylan or Andrew. I started second-guessing myself, *Is this plan such a great idea after all? Have I really heard from the King? Have we made all of it up in our heads? What are we going to do?*

"Raven," I whispered, "what's next? The guys have been gone a long time. What if they don't come back?"

"Ugh!" she sighed, "Unfortunately, Alli, I was just thinking the same thing. I don't know."

Suddenly, we heard footsteps on the path approaching us. Then, a whistle.

"Everyone, be quiet!" I barked. "Raven, shush the kids!" We hid behind the thicket.

"Here we go again!" Tom added sourly. I narrowed my eyes and glared at him. I couldn't help myself. Thankfully, my dirty look silenced him, so I could focus on who was approaching.

The footsteps drew closer, and I strained to catch a glimpse through the trees. I saw small flashes here and there but could not tell who was coming. The stranger was almost upon us, and my heart was racing. I held my breath for a few seconds in fear the noise of my pounding heart and shaky breath would give away our hiding place.

"Hellooo! It's me," Sir Reynald's lovely head popped over the bushes.

"Ahh!" A few cries arose from our startled group, including me. Although we were not expecting to see his face, we were completely relieved. My eyes met with Sir Reynald's, and I could no longer contain myself. I ran to him and fell at his feet.

"Oh! Thank goodness you are here! I've been so scared!"

"Alli," he soothed, "why didn't you use your trumpet, my lovely?"

"I...I...I...forgot," I stammered, for the first time in a long time. I hadn't stammered like that in weeks. I sat dumbfounded and overwhelmed. I gulped, resisting my need to cry.

"There, there, little one," Sir Reynald comforted, "I'm not mad at you. The Great King sent me to remind you of a few important things: who you are and what you have been given. There are more challenges ahead, and this is not the time to forget what to do."

"Yes, my Lord," I whispered. The others gathered around and joined me at his feet.

"Take heart! Have no fear!" he charged us, "The good King will see you through. But remember, things may look the darkest before the dawn." And with that, he was gone. In an instant, he disappeared.

"Now what?" Tom asked.

"We wait a bit longer, that's what," I replied. "Hey, do you guys remember the berries we ate when we first left the caves? Do you think we can find them again?"

"I don't know, but it is worth a try. I sure am hungry," replied Raven. "And we gotta feed these kids!"

So, off we went exploring the forest for the delicious berry bushes. We were amazed and excited to find them just a few yards from where we had been waiting. The small victory tipped our mood in a great direction. We grabbed handfuls of berries and eagerly ate them. Berry juice dripped from our chins as we celebrated. On our way back to our rest area, we were interrupted by sounds of laughter coming from the spot where Sir Reynald had been. We stopped in our tracks so quickly the children ran right into our backs.

"What was that?" I whispered.

"Let's take cover until we figure it out," Tom added. "There are some rocks over there!" He finally had a good idea! Breathlessly, we hid behind the rocks to see who or what was coming. I recognized Dylan's and Andrew's voices. Breathing a sigh of relief, I peered from between the rocks just to make sure it was them. I was surprised to see they were traveling with another person…Robin Hood? He wore a green cap with a feather sticking out its top, a long grey shirtdress, and green tights. The finishing touch to his garb was a bow and quiver full of arrows. I could tell he was the source of the laughter with his big smile and all.

"It's Dylan and Andrew. It's okay, everyone," I said as I motioned for the children to get up and come out of hiding. We ran over to them, and I couldn't help but stare at the man in tights, who stood in front of me.

"You must be Alli," he said as he bowed toward me. "And *you*…must be Raven," he said as he bent toward Raven, giving his hat a tip toward each of us. "And this," he said with a huge grin, "is my band of merry men!" He swept his hand back toward a ragtag group of travelers behind him.

Merry? They seemed anything but merry. I smirked.

He must have noticed my smirk because he said, "Don't let their faces fool you. It is not outward appearances that count. If you stick around these parts long enough, you will see things are not always what they appear to be."

He made a good point. I smiled; his words resonated with me. I remembered all the times I had seen the truth of his statement firsthand.

"This is Alan," Dylan introduced the stranger to us. "He offered to go with us since we lost our way."

"We didn't lose our way," I protested.

"Oh?" he said with his brow lifted. "Well, shall we say, you went...amiss?" Alan suggested.

"I know these woods very well. If you like, I can show you a safe way to get through them." He motioned toward the thick foliage overhead and the dense forest around us.

I looked at Raven and the rest of our small group for guidance. Their faces shone, and their eyes were bright with hope. Well, there was my answer. They seemed to like his offer.

"Okay. Let's go with him," I reluctantly added my acceptance of the man in tights. The whole situation made no sense to me. I never wanted to go back to the cave in the first place. I hated the thought of being back here. And now, with the new band of travelers, I wondered if the journey would ever end.

I need Saraiyah. Help! Help! Help! I felt so lost, like the first time I left the path and met that dirty snake. *Help me, Ima!*

"Alli, what are you thinking?" Raven's words interrupted my heart's cries for help. "You seem a million miles away. Are you worried about this guy?"

"No, I'm just wondering how we lost our way in the first place. I mean, I thought Prince Boqer and Saraiyah were leading us, you know? How'd we get so messed up? Now we're following some know-it-all clown in green tights."

Alan called out, "Hurry up, guys, we need to stick together. You never know what you'll find in these parts."

Feeling helpless, I sulked and watched skeptically. I was not sure we could trust this Alan guy. Truthfully, I wasn't sure about anything in this entire situation, but I silently marched onward. Alan's jolliness continued like a wind-up toy and seemingly spread to the others. His not-so-merry band of men started the journey looking as defeated and dismayed as I felt, but soon, their somber mood lightened, and their steps became lively. They exchanged light banter; one man even whistled as another man hummed. The lightheartedness even spread to the children, who ran and skipped along the way.

I remained skeptical, listening to as much of the men's banter as possible. I tried to grab little tidbits of their exchanges to learn more about Alan. From what I heard, most of the merry men had just recently joined Alan. They, too, had lost their ways. Apparently, he went around collecting lost souls in the forest. I chuckled to myself. This

Alan guy and his men reminded me of a Christmas story. But not just any Christmas story: *Rudolph the Red-Nosed Reindeer* (TV special), where Rudolph and Hermey go to the island of misfit toys. The amusing thought busied my mind, which was a good distraction.

After traveling for several hours, Alan informed us of a rest stop just ahead. He led us off the path to a spot by a small spring of water. I recognized the place. We had been there right after we fled the caves. I looked around and saw the rock table with the pitcher and basket of bread. Yep, for sure, this was the same spot.

"Hey! We've been here before!" Tom exclaimed, disgusted. "I hope we don't get lost again!"

"Not to worry, Milad," calmed Alan. "I know my way around these parts," he chuckled. "This will be a good place to stay the night."

Taking a break, we drank the refreshing purple liquid and ate our fill of the sweet honey bread. Alan directed, "Let's set up camp and turn in. We'll start again early in the morning." Without another word, Alan's band of men went to work: some grabbed fishing poles; others set up camp for the night.

"Come on, you guys, we can't let them do all the work," Dylan said. "Raven, do you want to take Tom and the kids to collect some wood? Alli, can you come with me to check out the area? I'd like to explore it more thoroughly than we did the last time we were here."

Andrew said confidently, "James, how 'bout we help

Alan's guys set up camp. Let's show them we aren't just a bunch of lost kids."

"Sounds great to me," James agreed.

THE CAVE AGAIN

"Okay, let's go," Dylan led us toward the large outcropping of rocks where we had camped the last time we were here. "I'm curious to see what is on the backside of these rocks," he continued as we navigated around the outcropping. We did not expect what we found—a very tall cliff face. The mountainside jutted high above us.

"The tree branches must've obscured our view last time. I can't tell how tall this is, but it sure seems *a lot* bigger than I thought!" Dylan exclaimed.

"Uh, for sure!" I replied in awe.

We continued down the narrowing path to the right, which ran along the creek. The water rushed along beside us. I marveled at the bright colors of the leaves; maybe the seasons were changing. Aspens and birches were shooting high above the path. Beautiful flowering bushes grew along the trail, sipping water with their dangly roots. You could get lost in the beauty of the place. Oh no! I'm *not* getting lost in anything around here!

"Maybe we should turn back soon," I offered but almost immediately noticed a rather curious crevice in the rocks to our left. I moved closer to check it out; Dylan followed close behind me. The crack was not a crack at all but a narrow opening.

"Dylan, could this be what I think it is?"

"I don't know; what do you think it is?" Dylan asked, his curiosity piqued.

"I think it is either a hidden entrance or maybe a cave-in of some sort," I said as I removed a few rocks from the opening.

"Are you sure you want to do that? What if it's been closed up on purpose to keep something bad from getting out? Or if it was a cave-in, you could make it worse."

"I'll go slow. I won't dig too much," I reassured Dylan. I knew I needed to keep moving the rocks for some unknown reason. "Come on, Dylan, help me move this big one." Despite a good effort from both of us, we could not move the boulder. We barely dislodged it. Just then, I heard a muffled groan from inside the crevice.

"Did you hear that, Dylan?" I asked frantically.

"What?"

"The muffled groan," I said, agitated.

"No. I didn't hear anything."

"Shh! Quiet! Listen!" I interrupted. The bossiness was coming back. After a few moments, there was only silence.

"Okay," Dylan said, sensing my concern. "Let's be super careful, just in case. We don't want to hurt anyone."

We removed the small debris with caution to give us a better angle on the big rock.

"How 'bout a large stick? Can't we use it as a lever?" I asked, not very confidently.

"Good idea! Give me a minute. I will search by the trees to see what I can find. I'll be right back. Don't move!"

Dylan went to the trees along the creek to find a lever, and I focused on listening at the small opening. While I waited impatiently, I heard another faint groan.

I couldn't contain my concern, "Hurry, Dylan!" I yelled, "I just heard another groan; someone's hurt!"

"Okay! I'm coming! I found a large branch!" He returned, dragging part of a fallen tree. We struggled a bit but finally wedged the limb under the large rock. Unfortunately, when we moved to the far end of the limb to apply force, it snapped without making any progress with the rock.

Exasperated, I said, "What are we gonna do?"

"Where's your trumpet?" I had forgotten all about my trumpet. Quickly, I pulled it from my bag. How had I forgotten about it *again*, especially after what Sir Reynald told me? Softly, I prayed, "O Great King! We need Your help!" I took a deep breath and blew the trumpet with all my might.

Back at camp, Alan stopped midstep as he heard the

trumpet's call. He intently gazed toward the horizon as if to pinpoint the source of the sound. "Alert! Someone is in distress!" he cried. He quickly took a headcount and realized Dylan and I were missing. "I need three volunteers to join me; Miss Alli needs our help."

Meanwhile, we carefully dug around the rock, trying not to freak out.

"Wait!" Dylan urged, "Shouldn't we wait to see the results from your trumpet? What if we make it worse in our rush?"

"You're right," I sighed, trying to calm my racing heart. "But I can't just sit here! There has to be something I can do."

"Well, what else do you have in your pack?"

"My journal, the King's Chronicles, and my bow and arrow," I replied.

"Why don't you read something to take our minds off this for a minute?" Dylan offered.

"Okay." I fumbled with my leather-bound book and opened it in the middle, where the poems and prayers were located. I tore a piece from the page and handed it to Dylan. Then I read aloud:

"Behold the King! Isn't He good?

Behold the King! He will take you through!

Riding on the clouds carried by the wind.

Behold the King! He makes life a breeze."

Although nothing changed on the outside, I sure felt calmer on the inside. The stress melted off with those powerful words.

Moments later, Alan and several men approached us. "What are you two up to?" he queried. We quickly got him up to speed, and he leaned in to assess the situation. He barked orders to his men and us. "You two, move back. We don't want anyone else getting hurt!" He reached inside a small bag slung over his shoulder. He pulled out two small vials: one with powder and one with oil. Being careful, he poured a thin line of powder across the base of the rocks blocking the entrance. Then, he lightly dripped some oil at each end of the powder.

"O Great King!" he stood back and proclaimed, "Come in Your power and Your name! Free the one who is trapped within!"

The moment his proclamation ended, the powder ignited and burned from each end with brilliant colors of magenta and gold. A sparking flame sputtered and burned down the line of powder until reaching its counterpart in the center. As soon as the sparks met, they flickered their last spark, *poof*...the rocks simply dissolved into powder. Just like that! They were gone! What in the world had I just seen?

Lying face down in front of us was a man, his bloodied hands outstretched as though he was trying to claw his way out of the cave-in. Alan quickly grabbed his waterskin and poured a small stream into the man's mouth. The wounded man sputtered and coughed, his eyelids blinking in the bright light. He moaned again, this time opening his eyes fully. He had scrapes and cuts on his head and hands and bruises on his face and arms. One of his legs was twisted and laid in a strange position.

"Thank, thank, thank you," he gasped.

"Where do you hurt?" Alan asked.

"My head hurts, and my leg is killing me," he mumbled and motioned toward his twisted leg. Without hesitation, Alan examined the man's injuries as though he was an expert.

"Men, carefully lift him and carry him down by the stream. Lay him in the small clearing, where the ground is soft. We can better address his wounds there." Alan's men responded swiftly and carefully. Several moans of pain escaped the man's tight lips as he was carried away. The cries of pain increased for a few moments as Alan set and splinted the man's leg. I couldn't help but cringe and look away. I felt so bad for the man.

"Alli!" Alan called. "Please come join us! Cleanse the scrapes and cuts with this healing oil," he said. As I joined them, he handed me another vial from his pouch.

"Please don't worry about me," the man groaned. "We were held captive. There are several others imprisoned deep within the cave. There was a posse of us on our way out when the cave-in happened. Please! Please! I implore you," he urged. "There are women and children trapped down there. They need your help!"

Upon hearing the news, Alan looked around at his men.

Without a command or word of direction, the men quickly tore some cloth from their tunics and soaked them in oil. Then they wrapped the oil-soaked rags on the end of a stick. They made a torch. Brilliant!

One of Alan's men, Richard, leaned in to question the man, "How did you escape? Where are the guards? Why were you the only one to get to the entrance?"

"But I wasn't the only one," he coughed. Alan offered him another drink. The man cleared his throat and continued to explain, "We were held captive for weeks. Recently, another group arrived and was imprisoned with us also."

"When did they arrive?" Dylan interrupted.

"Oh, about ten days ago, I suppose. It's hard to tell down there."

Ten days ago! That was when we got separated from our group! Hope ignited in me. The man had my full attention now. Could the other captives be our fellow travelers?

"The snake's wicked daimons tortured us. We had little food or water. Honestly, most of us had lost heart. We believed it was the end. But when the new band of prisoners arrived, our hope was renewed. Two of their leaders sang songs of praise to the Great King. The ground shook when we joined their singing, and our cell doors broke open. The snake's creatures scattered like rats jumping off a sinking ship. The leaders sent me out with a small team to ensure we were free of the enemy and secure an exit. I was almost at the opening when the cave-in occurred. The others must have been further behind me. I hope they went back for help."

Alan commanded his men, "Be on your guard! You never know what you might find. Weapons at the ready!"

RESCUE

I grabbed my bow and arrow from my pack, assembled it, and got up to join Alan's men. Alan started to protest but held his peace after one look at the determination on my face. Dylan jumped up beside me with his weapon in hand. We were ready.

"I'm not looking forward to going back in that cave, especially after the last time we were in one," I confessed to Dylan. "Did you hear the part about the new prisoners arriving right after we got separated from our group?"

"Yes, I heard that too. I know what you mean about the cave, but we've got to help them. Wouldn't it be great if some of the prisoners were our people?" I nodded my assent. I agreed with Dylan: we had to rescue them, or at least try.

We headed into the cave through the opening where we freed the injured man. There was only one torch for our band of five, so we stayed close together. The darkness and thickness of the air stirred up my anxiety; I couldn't get to where we were going fast enough. I just wanted to find the people and get out of here as soon as possible!

At last, we rounded a corner, and there they were! Many people were milling about in a wide area, much like the first cave had. Some were gathered around a small fire pit, while others were pacing back and forth. Several people in the group looked frail and emaciated like they'd been through the wringer. In total there were about fifty people.

"Alli! Dylan! Thank the King, you've come!" Rhey shouted. I was shocked and thrilled to hear his voice. I couldn't believe it was him, yet there he was, directly beside Prince Trueheart and several others from our group. They looked a bit worse for the wear and were a little hard to recognize. Their faces were smudged with dirty, dark-looking goo. But their excitement in seeing us lit up their eyes, breaking off the oppressive weariness. Our group was standing in the middle of all the prisoners. Prince Trueheart raised his right hand to quiet the clamoring noise. And it worked! He stood there with his hand raised, without saying a word—a hush fell on the crowd.

Prince Trueheart caught my eye; his gaze penetrated my thoughts. Where have you been? What happened to you? Why did you leave the caves? I heard his questions without him speaking a word.

"It was dark, we were scared, and we didn't know what to do or where to go," I quickly responded to his unspoken questions. The words tumbled off my lips quickly, one after the other. I told him where we had been and what we had been through. "We came back because it seemed like the right thing to do," I muttered breathlessly. I turned my gaze to my shoes, awaiting their rebuke. I knew I had really blown it. I messed up everything.

"Thank the King, you came back!" announced Rhey. "And thank the King, you left the caves. Who knows how much longer we would have survived down here." Shocked and consoled, I nodded to Rhey, thankful for his kind words.

Having cleared my throat, I introduced, "Prince Trueheart and Rhey, this is Alan and his band of merry men." The men tipped their hats to one another as a gentlemanly hello.

"We must get everyone out of here before we do anything else," Prince Trueheart declared. "Let's go!"

Relieved, Dylan and I gladly surrendered the lead to Prince Trueheart and Rhey. I was surprised: Alan did so as well.

Prince Trueheart and Rhey quickly gathered and organized the group and led us toward the mouth of the cave. A faint hint of Saraiyah's fragrance wafted gently amongst us. The noise and excitement rose and fell as we wound our way through the tunnel. At last, we could see the entrance! I was bursting with excitement. People celebrated as we spilled out the mouth of the cave into the glorious light of day!

After collecting the injured man and the men caring for him, we headed back to the clearing where Alan's remaining band of merry men were setting up camp. What a relief to have our whole tribe back together! I was overwhelmed with joy at the sudden turn of events. I felt light as a feather, and I wasn't alone in that feeling. Andrew's father was so excited to reunite with him that he playfully tousled his hair and led him to the stream for a man-to-man talk. Dylan's mother ran over and threw her arms around him in the biggest hug. Kids ran full speed into the arms of their parents as tears ran down their faces. Shouts of joy and laughter filled the air. Raven and I shared a joyous glance. We were beaming from ear to ear as we watched the teens and children reunite with their families.

In the distance, I noticed Mary, one of the little three-year-olds from our group, looking forlorn. Raven went over to help her and hold her hand. I walked over to join them.

"What's the matter, honey? Can't you find your mommy?" I asked.

"No," she said in her tiny voice. I looked at Raven and bent down to pick her up. I held her in my arms and surveyed the crowd. I hoped someone would recognize her, but everyone was caught up in their own reunions. No one seemed to notice us except Prince Trueheart. His tender gaze assessed the little girl. He knew something was wrong. I placed her gently on the ground as he came over and knelt next to her.

"Mary," he gazed tenderly as he spoke, "would it be okay if Alli held you on her lap?"

She nodded yes, and I gently placed her in my lap. "Mary, is your mommy's name Jenny?" Mary nodded again; her big eyes looked forlorn. "Your mommy has a very important job for the King. Your mommy has gone ahead of us to prepare our way to the King's castle. You see, honey, the special job the King gave her allows her to talk with the King in person. She tells Him the needs of our group. She speaks on our behalf until we find our way to our destination." Mary listened intently as Prince Trueheart continued.

Uh-oh! I knew what he meant. Her mom didn't survive. Just like my dad died and left me, so did her mom. *Poor, poor, little waif,* I mourned. Prince Trueheart and I locked eyes as I wondered if Mary was truly an orphan.

"Don't worry, dear Mary, you will soon be reunited with your Auntie B and Uncle Harry," he answered my unspoken question. Mary smiled at the very mention of her relatives.

"Can I go play?" she asked, bounding off my lap.

"Yes, of course!" he responded with a big smile. Mary ran off to join the others in a game of tag; I noticed one of the slightly older girls welcomed her sweetly. Children's ability to bounce back amazed me.

Prince Trueheart turned his attention to Raven and me, "Mary is going to need you for the next part of the journey. I believe you know what she is going through, Alli?"

"Yes, unfortunately, I do." I knew all too well the pain of losing a parent.

"Can the two of you accept responsibility for her until she can be reunited with her aunt and uncle?"

"Yes, we can share the responsibility. We'll do it together," Raven offered and grabbed my hand.

"Wonderful! Thank you!" Prince Trueheart turned away

and rejoined the others.

He made sure to assign everyone a task. I was relieved there were more of us now, including Alan, his merry men, and the other prisoners to share the tasks. I couldn't help but smile. I really had changed! The campsite was set up, the meals were cooking, and a certain rhythm returned to our group. Things were beginning to feel like they did before the first cave experience.

Later that night, we sat around the fire. We had just finished our first good meal in days: fried fish, fresh berries, and salad greens from the forest. I was grateful to have a full belly. Little Mary rested by my side as I listened to Rhey, Prince Trueheart, and Alan talk about the caves.

I found out that today's cave was the same cave we were lost in days ago. There were underground tunnels and chambers deep within the earth: a whole network belonging to the snake and his minions. We had been walking over the top of them the entire time, unaware.

"Saraiyah assured me in a dream last night that all who are present will be rescued," Prince Trueheart encouraged us. "I believe we can rest assured that we will be safe for the night. But we need to be on guard and take turns on the watch."

I looked down at precious little Mary resting. I couldn't help but wish she still had her mom. I stroked her hair with my hand.

"Alli, Dylan, and Raven," Prince Trueheart said. "Can you describe, in detail, everything you saw since we were separated?"

We each took a turn describing the happenings to our little group. It was interesting to hear the different perspectives of all we had seen and heard. Prince Trueheart and Rhey took it all in.

After our somewhat lengthy story, Prince Trueheart stood and called, "Everyone! Please, gather here with us! Raven, will you please lead us in song?"

"Yes, of course!" Her beautiful lilting voice lifted our hearts as soon as the notes hit the air. She sang:

"Who is this King of glory?

Do you know Him by name?

His ways are ne'er failing,

His love ne'er ending.

He beckons. Will you hear Him?

He's calling you by name."

When the song finished, Rhey thanked the Great King for our safety and our reunion. Then Prince Trueheart dismissed us, sending the reunited families to bed and the watchmen off to guard the perimeter of our camp.

Exhausted from the day, I quickly fell asleep and had the strangest dream. I was by a lake with Prince Boqer and Sir Reynald. They stood side by side and seemed so connected as if they were the same person. Like two sides of the same coin…heads and tails. Suddenly, a loud booming voice broke through the clouds. It said, "This is My loved son; He brings Me such joy!" Saraiyah was a dove flying above them. I recognized her by the beautiful, iridescent colors surrounding her and spilling off her wings. We were all traveling together on the path.

Instantly, the scene changed. We were *inside* the incredible castle on the mountaintop. I remembered the first time I saw the castle in my dream. In the distance, the Great King sat in brilliance on His throne. The scene was full of indescribable beauty. His appearance was so bright it was hard to distinguish His features. Was He human or something otherworldly? The throne was pure gold and surrounded by a sapphire blue sea, which flowed out of and around the throne. Creatures and children of all kinds surrounded the King. I recognized a few creatures, while others differed from what I'd seen, heard, or even imagined. The happy children giggled, laughed, and played around the throne. They didn't seem to have a care in the world other than playing. Every so often, a child would run up to the King with a gift: a pebble, a flower, a leaf. A few children brought drawings and artful scribbles. The King smiled and lovingly laughed with each child, no matter the gift. I could see how very much He loved them...*each and every* one of them.

I couldn't help but squint when I looked at the King: the light shining from His throne was blinding. I thought Saraiyah was bright, but the King was much more radiant. However, the children didn't seem to have any trouble; they were accustomed to the brilliance. I was taking it all in.

Then I heard Prince Boqer's voice in my head, saying,

"Would you like to meet My Father?" It felt completely normal for Him to speak this way. I replied yes in my mind. He motioned for me to approach the throne. I took a deep breath; trembling, I made my way toward the King's magnificent throne.

My eyes opened, and, on my way to the throne, I woke up. Although I was disappointed not to complete my journey to the throne, I lay perfectly still, not moving, wrapped in love, joy, and peace. I was soaking in the magic of the moment. What an extraordinary dream! One thing for sure: I couldn't wait to see Prince Boqer again. I liked how it felt being with Him. I could have laid there all day, but duty called. I got up and found my friends and breakfast.

Before we broke camp, Prince Trueheart and Rhey divided the travelers into groups. Prince Trueheart instructed, "It will be safer if we travel in smaller 'traveling tribes.' You will be less conspicuous to the enemy. Don't worry: we will rendezvous again before our final ascent up the cliff face to the King's palace." I let out a big sigh of relief. Boy, was I glad not to lead anymore!

"Miss Alli," Rhey interrupted my thoughts, "it's been decided that Dylan, Raven, and you will continue to lead your group. You have proven yourselves worthy guides."

"B...b...b...but," I sputtered, "doesn't the journey get more difficult the higher we go?"

"Yes," he replied. Before I could object, he continued, "This came straight from the King, Milady." He stared directly into my eyes.

"Trust Him!" I heard. Was Saraiyah speaking to me?

"The King has a special request, Miss Alli," Rhey continued.

"Yes?"

"Will you and Raven take Mary with you? She has become very attached to the two of you."

"Sure," I tried to muster a smile but sighed instead at the thought of this newest challenge.

"Remember: the King already knows what you need, Milady. Saraiyah will be with you," Rhey assured.

"She will?" I enthused.

"Yes, as she has been the whole time."

"Oh," I said, rather deflated. I hoped he meant she would be with me in person.

"Now, cheer up! You will do great! Plus, the adults will help you," Rhey encouraged.

"What? I'm supposed to lead the grown-ups, too?"

"Yes! Of course! Prince Trueheart organized your team. The parents of the teens from your group will be joined by their families, but the other children have reunited with their parents. Remember, Milady, the Great King believes in you!" And with that, he left for his next task. Gulping, I looked at Raven.

We decided it was a good idea to start with a list of our group members. The following had joined us: Dylan's mother, Ruth, and his little brother, William; Thomas's surly dad, Mitch, and his browbeaten mother, Lois; Andrew's mother, Elizabeth, and giggly twin sisters, Lily and Lila. Andrew's father, Saul, would join us further into the trip. Neither Raven's parents nor my mom would be on the journey, but we both had Mary with us. Lastly, there was James, who unfortunately was an orphan; he had no family to join us, which made me sad for him. But it's probably why he was so quiet. Or maybe he was just the silent type. I had to try and help him feel like he belonged more.

"By my count, we have four adults, four kids, and six teens," I concluded, "That's not so bad." Raven smiled, and her eyes shined.

"We'll be all right, Alli! You'll see!" she encouraged. I truly wanted to believe her.

BUNGEE JUMPING

Our small group was losing steam and losing it fast. We had traveled all day and made little progress. It took us forever to get to the base of the steep hill in front of us. Okay, it didn't take forever, but it did take the entire day. No one seemed to be in a hurry except for me. The parents were so happy to be reunited with their children they just wanted to play with them, which worked out great for the kids. All they wanted to do was play! All in all, nobody but me seemed to care about getting there. After all, I wanted to get home! At this point, I was tired of this whole world. Was I the only one that wasn't from here? Is that why no one else was bothered by the endless delays?

We trudged up the long hill in front of us. As we crested the top of the hill, the thunderous sound of a waterfall engulfed us. We couldn't tell where the sound originated from.

"Alli!" Dylan called. "Should we investigate?"

"Yes! Let's do it!" Raven enthused.

"Okay," I conceded.

We continued to the plateau at the top of the hill, and there it was: a breathtaking waterfall, over 400 feet above us, plunging down into the lake below. The lake had shades of blue and was crystal clear with light turquoise in spots. The water under the waterfall churned like a boiling pot while the rest of the lake rippled gently and peacefully.

"Can we stop here and rest for the night?" Raven pleaded, "The kids want to swim, and we have been traveling for hours. Maybe," she said with an impish smile, "*this* is the King's provision."

"Why not?" I shrugged and let out a sigh, "It's not like we're making any progress."

We gathered the rest of the group and set up camp on the plateau. Meanwhile, the children playfully splashed and swam in the lake. They were having a ball! I enjoyed the constant, comforting sound of the waterfall cascading down the cliff and tumbling into the lake. There was something for everyone to enjoy at this stop.

After we sat for a much-needed meal, Mary melted me with her big, brown eyes, "Alwie and Ravunnnn, Pah... lease, can we swim?" she pleaded. "I wanna swim."

Raven and I exchanged a knowing glance. How could anyone resist that? The other children called to us from the water.

"Okay! Okay!" we gave in. Raven and I wrestled off our cumbersome hiking gear and stripped down to our leggings and tank tops. We jumped playfully into the water with the kids. I couldn't help but migrate with our little group toward the waterfall: its pull was magnetic. Once we got beyond the bubbling and churning, the water was calm and still: peaceful even. It was like the effect of the power was peace and rest instead of turmoil.

Everyone was splashing and playing, having a blast, when suddenly, Thomas shot straight up like a rocket. All the way up the waterfall to the top! My head could not process what I had just seen!

From above us, we heard Tom shout joyfully, "Come on up, guys. Don't be afraid! It's great!"

Before I knew what was happening, *all* the kids were shooting up the waterfall to the top. *What's going on? How's that even possible?* I wondered.

"Alli! It's time!" I heard Saraiyah's voice whisper.

"Time for what?" I whispered back.

"Time for a leap of faith," she offered.

"A leap of faith? What do you mean?" I pleaded.

"Alli, it's time to surrender your will to the King completely. Trust in His goodness. The way you travel up the waterfall is to be like the children. They have childlike trust, and they trust the King."

"I don't understand, Ima!" I cried. Just then, I felt Saraiyah near me; her presence stilled my anxiety.

"Come now, Alli. It's time to go!"

Although it made no sense, I started swimming up the waterfall. I struggled under the weight of the water as it crashed on top of me. The water felt like a ton of bricks, weighing me down, keeping me from rising higher.

"Alli, *trust*! Daughter, you must trust to go higher."

"*Go low!*"

My mind repeated, *Go low*. Low was the exact opposite of where I wanted to go. I wanted to go up. Go low? I shrugged and decided to do it anyway, so down I went, I went low. Instantly, a flow of power that felt like a vacuum pulled me up. Quickly, I shot up the waterfall so fast I toppled over the ledge, laughing and landing on my bottom. Thomas, Dylan, Raven, Andrew, James, and the kids surrounded me on the ledge, everyone laughing heartily at my awkward arrival. From my sprawled position, I looked up at all my friends; my heart swelled with affection for them. The warmth in their eyes and the smiles on their faces made me think the feeling was mutual. I just sat there, enjoying the thrill of being there and the exhilarating way I arrived.

"Come higher, Alli!" Saraiyah called.

"Higher? How do I do that? What's higher? There's nowhere to go," I said, puzzled.

"Come up here, Alli. Look up!" Saraiyah directed. As I looked up, about sixteen feet above us, was a hint of another ledge. There was no waterfall to climb and no way to get up there. My eyes studied the rock face leading up to the ridge. I scanned for a path or a ladder, anything to get me there. After a few minutes, I discovered a narrow trail visible only for a few feet, and then it disappeared into the cliff face. How would I get up to the barely visible trail, let alone get up to the ledge?

The deep reverberating voice insisted, "You've got this! Trust us, Alli!"

"Is that you, my Prince?" I said, recognizing His voice. Determined to follow Prince Boqer, I moved forward, away from the group. The playful sounds of my friends and the group faded into the background. I was focused on one thing only: Prince Boqer. The one thing I desired was to be with my Prince. If He was calling me higher, I had to go. I walked into a cloud of mist and moved forward. Immediately, a step appeared in front of me, suspended in thin air. As soon as I set my foot on the step, another step appeared, hovering over the previous one. On and on, one by one, the steps continued to appear.

The top of the trail revealed a watery curtain flowing from the rocks above, hiding the ledge I sought. I felt drawn to go through the curtain of water. I had no idea what awaited on the other side, so I took a deep breath, held it, closed my eyes, and stepped through. I opened my eyes, and there He was! *There* he was! Prince Boqer's striking blue-green eyes pierced my heart with His love and beauty. I couldn't contain my excitement and ran to Him.

"Oh, my Lord!" I fell at His feet and cried, "Your love overwhelms me. I give my heart to You completely. Here I am, my Prince. I hold nothing back from You. I will follow You all my days. No matter what may come. Please, I ask this one thing, show me where to go and what to do. I trust

Your goodness. I really have learned You are good."

Prince Boqer chuckled with delight, "Oh, Alli! I love your heart! Believe and receive the life I bring! You are more important than you know. This moment of complete surrender is the moment where your life truly begins."

Immediately, the cliff and cave disappeared; we were in the King's palace. Prince Boqer led me down the hall to a small room. Only one furnishing was in the room: a gold, ornate, full-length mirror. "Alli, from this day forth, please remember this: what you see in the mirror is the real you. You are the daughter of the Great King!"

The image I saw took my breath away. I was startled by the reflection. The Alli I saw in the mirror didn't look like the Alli I knew. I was wearing an exquisite silver and sapphire embroidered dress. Somehow, the dress was made of real spun silver. It sparkled and shone in the light as if fully covered in diamonds. Even though I was in awe of my dress, the most shocking thing about the reflection was me: my face. I was beautiful! This was hard to admit. My thick, now deep auburn (no longer bright red) curls were held in place by two braids, tied gently in the back, and trailed down to my waist. Sapphire and silver ribbons were entwined in the braids. And a pièce de résistance sat atop my head: a simple diamond circlet, swirling with color and light, much like Saraiyah's crown.

After we exited the mirror room, Prince Boqer escorted me to the center of an opulent room. I recognized the beautiful room from my dream, the throne room. Once again, I saw the ornate throne. Prince Boqer announced, "Listen, everyone! Listen, all! From this day forth, I give Alli her new name. Alli, from now on, your name is Image Bearer because you bear the image of the Great King."

I stood in awe as the crowd erupted with cheers. Prince Boqer roared before me. I shook and vibrated as I received His energy, bravery, fearlessness, love, and joy. The best gift I received that day was His love. His love means everything! The crowd was cheering as a light fog rolled into the room. We were back in the shallow cave in the cliff, behind the waterfall, in a moment.

"Dearest Alli, it's time to go," Saraiyah said.

"Wait, please!" I threw my arms around Prince Boqer and buried my face in his mane. "Thank you for everything!" I cried. Tears rolled down my face, and I noticed a tear in His eye as well. He really loved me! Saraiyah directed me to a side opening at the cave back, leading to a ledge on the overhanging cliff.

"I love you so much, Alli," Saraiyah said as she gazed lovingly into my eyes. "Your time here is complete...for now. Here is your treasure-filled pack. It is time for you to fly and soar. Go now!"

Go? I questioned. *How do I go? Just do it; my heart belongs to the King, so I won't question His will. Okay, here I go!* Awe-filled, full of all that had happened, I stood silently staring at the water below.

I paused just a moment, Three! Two! One! I counted down, closed my eyes, and did a swan dive off the ledge of the cliff. Down, down, down! I fell like a bungee jumper. I was free-falling, waiting to collide with the force of the water below when...

HOME AGAIN, HOME AGAIN, TRA-LA-LA?

Whomp! I was not expecting to be instantly back in my room. I needed a minute to catch my breath. I sat up on my bed and looked around, drinking in every little detail of my room. *My!* It felt so good to be home. The moment became bittersweet, though, as I realized I would miss everyone immensely. Would I be able to bear it? I decided to push those thoughts aside. I'd think about them later. Right then, I wanted to do one thing…see my mom!

Hurriedly, I ran out of my room. "*Mom!*" I yelled. "Mom! Are you here? It's me. I'm back!"

"*Alli!* You're back! How are you?" Mom caught me in her embrace and held me close. She kissed my cheek and cried, "My girl! Oh, my girl! I have missed you!" She laughed as she gently placed her hands on my shoulders and extended her arms, "Let me have a look at you! I think you've gotten taller! You've certainly grown up! Are you hungry? Can I get you anything?" she chattered excitedly.

I was overwhelmed by everything, "Mom, I'd like to just take a shower and change my clothes. Meet you afterward to catch up. Okay?"

"Sure, baby. That's fine, just fine! Do what you need to do, and I will be ready when you are. My dear Alli, I love you so much! It is so good to have you home!"

I smiled and returned to my room. I gathered my clothes and towel for my shower and couldn't help but glance longingly at my desk, where I'd kept my Invitation. To my surprise, there was a letter on the desk: in its place was a scroll bound by a scarlet thread. I ran over to my desk and excitedly picked it up. As it unwound, immediately, the script confirmed it was from the King's realm! I tore into the words that glowed and vibrated, reminding me of the other world I grew to love. My eyes welled with tears as I read:

Dearest Alli,

Here are our answers to your unasked questions:

Yes, our love transcends time and space. It is available to you in both worlds.

Don't worry! Your journey isn't over. It has only just begun!

Many more adventures await you. Be on the lookout for them.

Remember, you are so loved and wanted.

Alli, we believe in you!

The Great King, Prince Boqer, Sir Reynald & Ima

As I read the note, I saw an excited Saraiyah in my mind, her sparks flying and colors shining everywhere. With a sneaky little grin, she said, "PS: there's a wonderful surprise awaiting you there."

I smiled and held the note close to my heart. What a treasure!

After my shower, I met Mom in our family room. She couldn't wait to hear about my adventures. She prepared a beautiful little celebration for us. On the table, beside my favorite comfy chair, were three delicate pink roses in a vase; Mom's fancy china plate (usually reserved for company only) filled with chocolate chip cookies, and my special cup full of Mom's delicious homemade piping hot cocoa. I jumped into my green, comfy chair and snuggled beneath my fluffy pink blanket. Mom had thought of everything! I felt so cozy!

Mom settled in across from me in her favorite "mom" chair. She looked so pretty against its floral print. She patiently sipped her chamomile tea, waiting to hear all about my journey. Meanwhile, I was relishing the homemade cocoa and the delicious cookies. Boy! I had really missed these! Most of all, though, I had missed my mom. I was ecstatic we were back together.

I took a breath and shared my story with my mom between cookie bites. I told her about the trumpet and all the gifts I'd received. I spoke about the things I did, especially the things I didn't want to do but did anyway. I gushed about Saraiyah and her incredible beauty. Most of all, I shared how much I loved the people, Prince Trueheart,

Sir Reynald, Prince Boqer, Rose, and Rhey...all of them. I really loved them all. Lastly, I told her about my incredible time with Prince Boqer and my new name. Everything—from start to finish. We laughed and cried together. I didn't hold anything back, which kind of surprised me. I never really opened my heart to my mom like that before, and it felt so good.

I told my mom my dream about the Great King on His throne and the beautiful creatures. I wanted her to know about it all. I was so excited I talked for hours. I kept remembering more and more details about my journey. I loved telling her everything and how intently she listened. She seemed to hang on to every word. She even belly laughed when I told her about my first impression of Raven. In fact, we both laughed, but I couldn't keep from getting choked up as I spoke about her.

I confided, "Mom, Raven and I became best friends. I've had a *real* best friend, and I'm already missing her so much!"

After I finished sharing my stories, I pulled out the note. I had tucked it between the seat cushion and the arm of the chair. "I found this note on my desk, where I used to keep the invitation," I said and handed the note to her.

"This is so special, Alli!" she said after reading the words. "It is hard for me to describe the happiness I feel when I read this. I think this will stay with you for the rest of your life! I am so happy for you!" she exclaimed. "Do you know what your surprise is?"

"I don't know, Mom. I just don't know," I sighed slowly.

"I sort of guessed it might be something to do with us, but I am not sure. I know, at the very least, it will be awesome!" She agreed.

"Mom, after all this, I have one big question for you."

"You do? What's your question, honey?"

"Why did you tell me my journey would happen while I slept here but didn't tell me I would end up being in a totally different world? As a matter of fact, how long have I been gone?"

"Well, you were gone, um, let me see," she paused while she calculated, "for two weeks ten hours and thirteen minutes."

I laughed at her preciseness. "Incredulous," I said. "That's all? How's that possible? It felt like I'd been gone forever, well, months really, or a month at the very least. I've only been gone the time I usually spend at the summer camp. That must've worked out if you had to explain my absence to the neighbors, eh?"

Mom answered, "First of all, I didn't disclose you would be in a completely different world because I knew it would be too much to absorb. I also knew that once you got going, you would do great! I know you are amazing and the Great King would equip you for the journey. The last part is science I don't understand. I believe it has to do with quantum entanglement and quantum physics."

"Oh, is that *all*!" I grinned. "Makes sense, though." We laughed as we finished our snacks.

The next day, Mom sent me to the nearby corner store to pick up a few groceries to hold us over until our big shopping trip on her payday. At the store, I went down the card aisle to find something special for my mom. I was so grateful for her support. I knew she'd been praying for me, but more than anything, I wanted to thank her for being my mom. I appreciated and loved my mom more than ever. Now, I needed a card to tell her how much.

As I studied the cards, intent on finding the perfect one, I was astonished to hear, "Alli? Alli? Is that really you? Are you kidding me!"

I recognized the voice and froze in shock. What if I turned around and it wasn't her? "Alli?" the voice persisted. I slowly turned around.

What happened next was more than anything I could have dreamed of. There she stood in front of me, the girl with the prettiest, sparkling, deep blue eyes and black hair. There she stood! My best friend—Raven! My jaw dropped so hard I thought it would hit the floor. I looked around quickly, wondering if I had stepped back into the other world. Nope! My eyes focused on our surroundings. I was still in the corner store in my hometown.

I stood frozen in disbelief, but Raven didn't hesitate. She came over and threw her arms around my neck, locking me in a giant bear hug. We both laughed and cried as the realization of our reunion hit us. I hugged her tightly; unlike my previous nature of recoiling from a hug, I leaned completely into this one.

"What a dream come true! Do you really live here in

Wondersville? I live here too!" I exclaimed. "After I got back, Saraiyah and the King left me a note on my desk. The note said I had a surprise coming to me. I had no idea what it was!" I stared right into her beautiful eyes and said confidently, "It's you, Raven! You're my surprise!"

"Do you wanna grab a pop and sit outside for a few minutes?" Raven asked excitedly.

"Yes!" I gushed. "I know Mom won't mind. She will be so excited! She was eager to see what surprise the King had for me."

We sat outside the corner store, sipping our drinks and letting the last few moments sink in. We were there, together, in the same world, in the same hometown. It was almost unbelievable. We tried to figure out why we hadn't discovered these facts in all our conversations. We finally chalked it up to how busy we had been with all the adventures. I told Raven I had a sneaking suspicion Saraiyah intentionally kept us from knowing until now. And not knowing sure made this moment incredibly sweet!

I hesitated. "Do you think we can stay friends like we were in the other world?"

"Oh! For sure! Of course! Are you kidding me? Don't you think that was the whole point? I mean, it's no accident we both live here." Raven continued, "In fact, I think we are gonna have many, many more amazing adventures together."

"Really? You do?" I asked hopefully. I slowly sighed. With all my heart, I hoped she would say yes. I just knew

I couldn't go back to the dull, boring rut I was in before I received my invitation.

Raven took my hand, locked eyes with me, and enthusiastically said, "Yes! Trust me, Alli, I know we will! And you know what…it's gonna be great!"

The End